I0694330

Written By

Sharon K. Angelici

Write with Light Publications
Colorado, USA

ISBN: 978-1-7378158-4-6
ISBN: 978-1-970289-02-2

Library of Congress Number: 2023931864

DEDICATION

To and for the people in my life who stayed when this straight presenting person told you she was gay. I wouldn't be here without your love and support. ; My story isn't over yet

To Taylor & Gabe who've helped bring it all together

For tulips in spring

CHAPTER 1

"Oh holy hell, please don't let it be December again."

Her hand fished around inside the size twelve rubber boot. It wasn't her boot, just the one they used for the Widows and Orphans fundraisers and for special occasions like today's calendar selection. Sixteen of the firefighters were eligible, and although she'd been in every calendar, she only wanted one of the last two months left in the boot, and she didn't want December, not again. The pieces of paper tickled her fingers, and she sent her best lucky wish to choose the right month. She rolled each paper, trying to feel the letters, dropped the longer of the two, and pulled out her hand. She turned it over, and both arms shot into the air.

"June, baby!" She held up the folded piece of paper and danced around like a child, her dark curls flipping and flopping with an embarrassing, jagged motion. "Hell yeah!" She pumped her arm. "I don't have to wear that stupid candy cane furry Santa suit." Her dance was awkward and silly, but the celebration was real.

Lester reached into the boot and pulled out the last slip, knowing before he opened his piece of paper what the outcome was. "Well, kiss my ass." He turned it around to reveal the word "December."

"Aww, don't be so sad, big boy." She punched his thick shoulder. "The chicks dig a guy in red." Ella covered her mouth to hide the laughter as she repeated the conciliatory phrase he'd used on her last year. No one in the fire house wanted to be December.

"That's cold, Cinder Girl." He stuffed the piece of paper into his pocket. "Some of us can't pull off that red velvet crop top."

"Oh, Soot-boy, if you want my red velvet, you'll have to work harder than that." She ran her hands down the front of her uniform shirt. "That's just so sad." She shimmied her hips. "I guess it's lucky I've got June to keep me nice and warm."

She clapped her hands, and like flipping a switch, the bells on the wall rang through the building. Their rivalry over the fundraising calendar came to an abrupt end.

"Damn!" she yelled as the alarm blasted through, ending her dance. Ella was on her feet in seconds, running toward the voice, calling the command for the station's on-duty roster.

"All units, all units report to 3303 Fellows way. Stations sixteen and forty-nine are already on scene."

Ella stepped into her gear, snapping one shoulder suspender after the other as the turnout pants snugged onto her nearly six-foot frame. Immeasurable amounts of water were in her future, as well as the blazing heat of flames. This was her armor, not as deflective as a knight on a white horse, but protective enough as a member of station house eight eighteen.

She pulled her dark curly hair into a sloppy ponytail as she took her position beside Lester Feller, her best friend and long-term wingman. "Good to go, Feller?" she asked as she slipped her headset into place.

"Roger that, Eastman!" His hazel eyes were wide and enthusiastic as he flipped switches to activate the lights and sirens.

"Good to go, Probie?" she yelled to Sebastion Wilson, the newest team member, and the best he could give was a thumbs up as the pumper truck tore from the station. Ella knew that confidence took time for probationary firefighters. She hoped that would be true for this kid.

The team arrived on the scene to a fully engulfed warehouse surrounded on all three sides by vacant grassy fields. The units already on scene were working to contain the brush fire.

"Easy as pie. It's just a little baby fire," Feller said as he hopped to the ground. "We could do this one with a sandwich in each hand."

"Dude, no!" Ella yelled back. "Don't say shit like that."

"Come on, Cinder."

She wrinkled her nose at his playful nickname for her; Ella, the fire killer, was always hot for the girls and cold for the flames. It was a cold night in high school when she swaggered in, dressed to impress, dark curls tied up on her head, frayed jeans tight to her thighs. Paige Turner had been sitting on the felled tree beside her. Ella had been given a single task: to maintain an already burning fire. That was her job. The fire wasn't raging, but it was high enough to keep the party goers warm, and all she had to do was add a log and fuel the flames.

Destiny called her to be a firefighter that night. It was clear when, less than twenty minutes later, she'd reduced the blaze to a pile of ash and cinder. That paired with the name Ella, and the endearment almost made itself.

"Don't play that card, Feller," she said. "Nothing's easy 'til it's done."

He reached to pull the hose free from the truck, and before he extended it to its full length, she had it connected.

Probie was opening the hydrant, and they were blasting the flames with water.

They were a tight team, the two of them: Ella Eastman and Lester Feller, Cinder and Soot.

~~~~~~~~~~~

"Easy as pie," she muttered, shimmying out of her turnouts. As she walked toward the locker room to shower off the saturated stench of smoke and grit, she added, "You're such an ass."

"Come on," Lester said, "buildings collapse all the time, Els."

She tossed her uniform top into the hamper and flipped her t-shirt and bra in one quick motion toward her open locker. Ella didn't care about her looks or who looked at her in the station house. This was her family, and Lester had seen her naked more than anyone on the planet. She didn't understand how she could be a firefighter, a queer female, and single. That combination was a mighty trap for the thirsty. Turning thirty in two months was sobering, especially considering her circle only included her station house family and her TV fandom friends. She wasn't alone, but she was perpetually lonely.

"*Buildings collapse*," she whispered as she yanked the handle to open the flow of shower spray.

She loved that long burst of cold water just before the pulsating heat. It reminded her she was alive, and after the barrage of debris they'd just endured, she was happier for it tonight. Bits of ash tinted the water as her fingers combed through. The dark pool around her feet was confirmation that this was not a "sandwich in each hand" kind of job.

"Could have been worse," Lester said a few minutes later to the steel shower wall barrier between them.

Ella's back arched, tipping her hair into the stream of water. Her fingers pulled the shampoo suds away. She relaxed into the sensation of water running over her breasts, along the
~~~~~~~~~~~

rips of her abdomen, across her unshaved sex, and down the flex of her thighs. All senses alive and well, she heard Lester's words. *Could have been worse.*

"That's not a great motto for a firefighter to live by, you know," she told him.

"It's working out just fine for me."

"You scare me, Soot-boy."

She turned the water off and tugged the towel around her body. His behavior was casual to the point of reckless, but that had always been his way. She had another eighteen hours to continue this conversation, and then she would relax for two glorious days. She needed every minute of that time to finish work on her project. This was her year, she knew, as she thought about leather, vinyl, dabs of fabric glue, and the *Blasphemers'* Dracea Barnes.

"What do you think about this one?" Morgan Hail asked as she set the lamp in the plastic tote.

"It's ugly as hell, Morg." Beatrice grinned as she put four glass platters in her own tote. "That will for sure enrage a customer, but does it really matter?"

"It all matters, silly." Morgan reached to scratch the freshly shaved stubble on her new undercut. "We're raging! We want people to come angry and leave chilled."

"You really are an artist, aren't you?" Beatrice rolled her cart toward the next overflowing dumpster behind the shopping plaza.

"Everything we get from here is going to a great cause, but it still has to have function."

Beatrice held up a two-foot tall blue vase. "Jackpot!" she yelled as she pumped it over her head like a first place trophy.

"That one's super nice." Morgan fished out three chipped coffee mugs and a plastic camping table. "Why do they throw such good shit away?" The question was mostly rhetorical as she tugged the zipper on her jumpsuit tight to her chin and pitched her five-foot-four-inch frame into the dumpster for a full body dive.

It was early morning. Her legs felt strong this time of day, so she kicked through the bags of paper and trash. Her foot hit something hard, and she scooped the plastic bag aside and pulled up a fire extinguisher. The gauge on the side read "Empty," and she took it. In her line of work, she could use just about anything.

She dropped the treasure over the dumpster wall and onto the ground and declared, "So much good shit."

The service door to the used goods store swung wide just as Morgan hoisted her body up, heaved one leg over, and lowered herself to the ground.

"Hey Max." She waved to the kid in the striped apron.

"Mor—gan." He drew her name out with a hipster trill and pointed at the security camera. "Boss says he's got three huge bowls for you." He leaned his entire body against the door, propping it so she could come inside.

"Really?" Her grey eyes opened wide, and she didn't hide her excitement as she picked up the broken extinguisher, brushed off the sticky paper, and set it on the rolling cart. "That's so great."

"You know you're kinda weird." His smirk was slick, and even though she dated along the full spectrum of humans, Max was always a jerk to her. She wouldn't give him a first glance, let alone a second.

"You know you're kind of a douchebag." She picked up the box on the floor just inside the door.

"I've heard you say that, but at least my girlfriend exists. Where's yours?" He didn't wait for an answer, because he didn't really care.

What bugged her most was that he had a valid point. Morgan hadn't been on a date in months. In her defense, if she needed one, she didn't have time for dinners and movies. She had goals and falling in love wasn't something that fit into her immediate plans.

Art was the plan. It always had been. In a perfect world, Morgan's ink, paint, and charcoal would be the only things her hands would touch. But her world wasn't perfect, and as much as she wanted her sketchpad to pay all the bills, it didn't, not yet. "These bowls are going to splinter like crazy!" she yelled to Beatrice as she exited the building.

"Distance high five!" Beatrice yelled back.

Morgan put the box on her cart. There was no shame in her game because dumpster diving kept customers coming back. Every temporary treasure was a booking on the schedule and a patron in her rage rooms. For now, shattering trash was a one-way ticket to the future.

CHAPTER 2

"Come on, Les. It's tomorrow, man," Ella yelled into the speakerphone, balancing at a gravity defying angle on the arm of the chair. She was burning the threads on the seams of her vinyl suspenders with a mini butane torch, putting the final touch on the costume that had consumed every moment of her free time for the last two months.

"Sorry, Els, the lady comes first. You'd tell me that if you had one."

His cocky laugh was frustrating and insulting, but that truth hurt. She'd love to share her life with someone, but not just anyone, and her obsession with the *Blasphemers* TV show was a quirk most women just didn't understand.

"Not when I've spent hundreds of dollars on VIP access and weeks on my cosplay. You're such a filthy asshole, Lester." She slid the pants across her lap, checking for loose threads or anything that would diminish the integrity of the costume. Her elbow hit the table, knocking the 3D printed grenades onto the floor.

"Can't do it, Cinder. You're just going to have to be the Arsonist all by yourself. "

"Fuck." She swore into the phone, not because he was letting her down, but because she'd just lit her finger on fire trying to catch the grenades.

"Come on. Give me a break. Don't be that mad."

"Oh, it's not…It's not you. Well, it is kinda you, but I just burned my finger on the torch trying to juggle falling grenades." She walked to the freezer in the kitchen and pulled out a lightweight ice pack. She twirled a towel around the bag and pressed the cold bundle to her finger.

"Are you sure you're a firefighter?" He laughed.

"Kiss my ass. If you weren't distracting me, I'd have been just fine!" she yelled across the room, knowing that the speakerphone would pick up her voice.

"I really am sorry, Els. Keep all my VIP perks. Maybe you can use my photo ops to meet what's-her-name?"

She was flipping her middle finger, which he couldn't see or hear. "Dracea Barnes. Her name is Dracea Barnes, and I already have a pass for her, you jerk."

"Well, now you've got two. And if you were trying to convince me to cancel my weekend, calling me a jerk is the worst way to do it."

"Yeah, yeah. Well, you're supposed to be my wingman." She huffed.

"Maybe next year. I'll see you at work on Monday." He ended the call before she could respond.

"Jerk!" she yelled as she looked at her blistering finger. "Some firefighter for sure," she mumbled as she held up the full length rubber pants. Best cosplay ever.

Ella opened the first aid kit and sat at her kitchen table. The small cottage wasn't spacious, just an open-air kitchen and living room with a small bathroom next to a bedroom that was just large enough for a double bed and side table and a second room for her cosplay and TV obsession. She hoped one day to share the space with someone special. She just hadn't met them yet.

She slathered the burn with cream and wrapped it tight. *Cut out the oxygen and nothing will burn.* She repeated the phrase from the first aid class she'd taken in high school. She never understood why, of all the things they'd discussed in class, fire and burns stuck out above everything else.

As she packed up her medical bag, she stared at the ticket vouchers on her table. "Fuck it," she said as she readied herself for the convention she'd waited a lifetime to experience.

~~~~~~~~~~

The alarm buzzed at five a.m., and Ella rolled over. She'd had a difficult time falling asleep with the burn and the leaky melting ice pack, but now that morning had arrived, she was out of bed in a heartbeat. The spandex pants slid over her thighs, muscles hard from powerlifting five days a week. She wasn't a gym rat, or so she thought. She was more concerned about carrying victims from raging infernos than impressing potentials with her biceps.

She liked what she saw reflected in the mirror, but she was more than that. Being fit was part of the job, and if she felt good in a sleeveless shirt, that was a bonus. She'd carried most of the costume in the trunk of her car, basing that on her last experience of driving in costume, which hadn't played well on her social media page.

"Firefighter caught with her pants up" was the tag Les put on the post. On her way to a cosplay event, the fake bloodstain on her shirt caught the attention of a part-time security guard at the truck stop and, before she could explain, she was getting first aid from an overzealous rent-a-cop. She could still hear the raging laughter in the video as Les tried to steady the camera. @Cinder_EllaE became an internet sensation
~~~~~~~~~~

for about five days, but the screen captures lived in infamy on the corkboard wall at the station house.

Ella double and triple-checked every piece of the costume before folding it into the trunk of her car. The vehicle, her baby, was a vintage powder blue Buick Electra, restored by her grandmother's life partner, Lou. She loved the vehicle, with its sharp lines leading to the tail flares. It was a one of a kind ride, and although Lou's passing was bittersweet, the memories of them driving together with the top down were some of the first she could recall with clarity after losing her parents.

"Ready to roll, Charlene." Ella rubbed her hand across the dash. She'd changed the stereo for a hands free operation, making it safe in an emergency, but everything onboard was just as she had inherited it. The car didn't answer back, but Ella knew she was ready.

The Blacktree Comic Palooza convention was a traveling event. Unlike the national cons that took place in the same city every year, a *palooza* by name was never in the same place twice. This year it was less than ten miles from Ella's cottage, and without airfare and hotel rooms, VIP access was finally affordable, and she was excited about the bonus experiences.

Her event pass came with daily parking, and although it was at the convention center, the spacious location put her assigned space two walking blocks from the VIP entrance. With the top snugged in place on her convertible, she listened to music through her trunk as she zipped, clipped, and buttoned her way into the costume. As a full-time firefighter, she chuckled as she tied the 3D printed mask over her face and clipped plastic pipe bombs and grenades to her bandoleer one at a time.

Ella's grandmother would not embrace this passion for the sci-fi series about a group of vigilante outlaws hell bent on destruction, especially a real life firefighter who cosplayed as The Arsonist. Ella felt the blistered skin of her burn as she checked the thumb battery before tugging the cuffed black glove over her hand.

"You are a badass, Ella Eastman," she whispered to herself as she tucked the car key into the rubberized utility belt around her waist. She'd spent an extra day making the pouches usable instead of just a faux prop.

Before she had a chance to turn around, she heard, "Sweet costume, dude!" It was some random guy yelling from across the street. Her mask hid her satisfied smile. Ella was actually enjoying the walk to the entrance.

Another guy yelled, "Blasphemers For Life!" It was a funny catch phrase used by hardcore *Phemers*, the nickname given to fans of the show, *The Blasphemers*. In the full outfit, no one would recognize Ella, and that was okay with her. @Cinder_EllaE could move freely amongst the crowd until the costume contest tomorrow.

She walked two blocks to the convention center and enjoyed the constant praise of con-goers. The line for entry was long, and security checks were awkward as the officers spent extra time flexing weapons, looking down plastic gun barrels, and safety tying anything that could cause legitimate harm.

"Are you entering the contest?" the blue feathered alien creature behind her asked.

Ella turned to look at the person who felt half her six foot height but almost as wide in billowy flowing feathers. "I haven't decided yet. You think it's good enough?" Ella had already registered for the contest, mostly because of how many hours she'd spent making it. She thought it was a great representation of the character, but she was also her own worst critic.

"You'll win for sure," the security guard interrupted. "I've frisked about three dozen Arsonists already, but dude, yours is top-notch! Best I've seen."

The surrounding crowd all seemed to agree. Ella felt a rush of excitement, confirming that coming alone might not have been so terrible after all.

She spent the first hour picking up her VIP badge and special event add-ons, reading through the glossy sixteen page schedule, and marking off every *Blasphemers* panel she wanted to attend. She matched her advanced ticket with the meet and greet session for the cast. At two thirty tomorrow, she would meet the one and only Dracea Barnes, the actor who played the Arsonist. Ella had been dreaming about the opportunity since the series premiered three years ago. This was going to be the best weekend of her life.

"Come on, buddy! Green means go!"

She pushed the center of her steering wheel, reminded instantly that the horn was a button on the floor. Morgan hated borrowing the retired delivery truck, but it was the only vehicle in her group of friends that could manage inventory for the convention. Her legs cramped from the flex on the gas pedal and lack of cruise control. Morgan knew that an occasional extra walk might improve her strength and flexibility, but you can't sketch taut-chested Amazonian sapphics on a five-mile hike.

Her cheeks puffed air to blow the stray piece of lime green hair from her eyes. The day after her new undercut, she'd bleached the length on top and added the green. This was going to be her best artist's alley sale ever. Traffic was heavy three blocks from the convention center, and she followed the signs around the back for "deliveries only." The grey-haired man at the gate grumbled as Morgan rolled down her window. He stared at her hair longer than was considered polite.

"Artist, right?" He held his clipboard, ready to check off the name.

"Morgan Hail, HailStorm and R.A.T.S. Studio." She said and waited as the gatekeeper ticked his pencil tip beside the name on the list. He folded the sheet over to the second and then third page.

"You've got booth C20." He didn't look up. "Wear this in the vendor hall at all times. You'll need it to get in and out all weekend." He passed a laminated badge with her vendor information displayed beneath the Blacktree Comic Palooza convention logo.

"Okay." She waved her clipboard at him. "Where should I park?"

"Someone is there to help you unload in bay 16 and you get parking spot 68 for the run of the event." His answers were monotone and robotic, and at two-thirty in the afternoon, he had a long way to go to check in the more than two hundred vendors for the event.

"Thank you, Gregg." She noticed the use of two *G*'s and wondered why the second was necessary. Five-year-old Gregg probably had it easy when learning to spell his name in kindergarten, three letters, easy peasy, or maybe his mother wanted him to stand out in the crowd of one *G* Gregs.

Morgan pulled the delivery truck to the unloading bay, not to be confused with the loading bay that she would use Sunday morning to accomplish this task in reverse. Hopefully with empty containers replacing the overstocked bins of artwork she aspired to sell.

"You need any help with that?" the attendant asked as they jumped off the loading dock ramp.

"I'd love some help." Morgan held out her hand. "Thanks, Britt." The name tag had a place for pronouns, and Britt with two T's used she/her. "My name's Morgan, she/her, also." The handshake was slow and warm, and she wondered if Britt might like to meet up for a drink.

"Nice to meet you, Morgan. Put your badge on. What's your booth number?"

"C20," Morgan said as she fastened the vendor identification to the lanyard and dropped it around her neck. Before she could ask another question, Britt was stacking boxes on a flatbed cart and walking away with thousands of dollars worth of paintings, prints, and products created to catch the eye of any and every *Blasphemers* superfan.

Morgan loaded her personal hand cart and attempted her very best jog-walk to catch up with the fast-paced Britt.

"C20, here you go. Do you have any more?" She folded the cart into half the full size and pushed it out of the way.

"Maybe one more load." Morgan smiled as she answered.

"Great, I'll grab that load, and you can go park your truck. Security is here for the rest of the con, so your stuff is safe. Get to know your table neighbors if you're here alone or you'll never get to pee." She was walking away as she shared the information and didn't care about Morgan's response. Clearly, she was busy and had no interest in making a connection.

"Thanks, I guess." Morgan mumbled mostly to the backside of the elusive yet attractive Britt.

The rest of the afternoon was consumed with folding tables, crates of plastic covered art pieces, and strategically draped velvety purple fabric. Morgan admired her artwork, which primarily focused on the first season of characters she enjoyed from *The Blasphemers*, a few other long running sci-fi series, and character cards that were mostly commissions. A supposed friend, the Arsonist, torched her favorite character, Bruiser, and after the season finale, Morgan couldn't continue watching. Bruiser was the character she most identified with, the muscle of the group who also loved to crochet for the innocents left in the vigilante Blasphemous wake.

"My sweet Bruiser," she whispered as she set her favorite print on the easel. Morgan displayed hundreds of postcard sized color sketches of the over fifty poster sized pieces she sold in the small gift shop she owned. Art was life, along with a side gig that was her real money maker. This artist had no intention of starving.

"Your work is nice," the vendor beside her said. They had a display of leather goods, practically impractical reproductions for cosplayers. Morgan recognized the 3D printed Arsonist flame gun and grenades buckled into a leather harness. The attention to detail was impressive.

"Thanks," Morgan replied as she sorted through her emotional disconnect from the use of the word.

"Nice" is bland. It's what you say when you don't know what else to say, and it always hit her artist soul hard. She knelt below the level of her table to avoid continued conversation. Tomorrow, they'd have endless hours to talk about the event. Tonight she wanted to set up her space. A convention so close to her neighborhood was rare, so she was happy to drive home and sleep in her own bed. Tomorrow she'd meet fans from around the globe, and she hoped a certain percent of them would gobble up all of her work.

~~~~~~~~~~

The following morning, Morgan was glad that she'd made a thermos of coffee. She hadn't planned for the foot traffic around the venue, and by the time she parked the truck, she had twenty minutes to spare. VIP ticket holders got a one hour window of priority access to the vendor hall. That meant two hundred and fifty people didn't have to push and shove their way through the football field sized venue.

"Cash box, notebook, coffee." Morgan double checked her bag and looked in the oversized side mirror. "And a happy artist smile." She laughed as she slipped her badge over her collar and pressed it to her chest. She clapped her hands together for a pep talk. "You got this, Morgan Hail. Let's do this!"
~~~~~~~~~~

CHAPTER 3

"Can I take a picture with you?" If the girl was ten, Ella would have been surprised, but the squeaky tone of her voice, and the hastily made Arsonist costume, was enough to make Ella's heart melt.

The VIP entrance had a short line, and Ella was barely ten feet inside the venue building when the girl abandoned her mother and ran up to touch Ella. She dropped to one knee, and her costume pants made a crackly, squeaking sound beside the girl's ear. Little hands touched the fake explosives clipped to Ella's bandolier, and they bounced against her chest one by one.

"What's your name?" Ella asked with a deep voice meant to sound like the character but also to disguise herself.

The child scrunched her tiny face and answered with the most adorable forced grumble, "The Arsonist." She waved her pretend flamethrower to imitate the opening credits and write the name of the show in front of them.

Ella found it strange yet adorable, and she was glad the mask covered her face, hiding the giggle as she forced a grumbly, "That's my name, too. Maybe we're twins." Ella made a fist with her gloved hand, and the grappling movement activated the battery operated flame in her thumb. The effect wowed the child and made convention participants stop to watch the interaction.

"That's—so—cool." The girl bumped her fist against Ella's, and the adult accompanying the child snapped the picture with her phone's camera.

"Thanks a lot," they said almost at the same time, and Ella thought that so far it might be the best part of the day.

The girl touched Ella's glove. "How did you make that?" She broke from pretending to be the Arsonist, allowing her curiosity to come through. "I would do that to mine if I knew how."

Ella laughed. "This is just a Halloween light you can get for pumpkins. Every store will have them in September." Ella stood to talk to the adult. "If you follow my posts on social media, you can see all of my other secrets and tips." She opened the pouch on her belt and took out her phone. The pad on her finger allowed her to activate the touch screen to share the download code for her account. The adult logged in and swiped through until she got to Ella's page.

"@Cinder_EllaE. This is you?" She held the screen for Ella to see, and the most recent close-up image of the thumb-light mechanism appeared..

"Yep, that's me."

The adult turned the phone so the little girl could see the photographs. "Are you a real fireman?" she asked.

"I am a real fire*fighter*." Ella whispered. "I enjoy putting fires out, but, shh. That's our secret."

"Wow, mom." The girl's mouth was open wide, and Ella felt a sense of empowerment move into the pixie of a girl.

"See, Cali. We can be anything that we want."

Cali was thunderstruck, and it took a long moment for her to snap back to the conversation.

"Is your name Cindy?" the mother asked, basing the question on the posted username.

"Well, actually, my name is Ella, but I don't just share my secret identity with everyone." She winked at the mother, but the woman couldn't appreciate the expression through the mask. Ella seized the pause in conversation to eye the woman up and down. In full costume, the appraisal was discreet.

The mom swiped through Ella's profile. "She has over two hundred thousand followers, Cal. So make sure you keep it super secret."

"Wow." It was the last thing the child said before she ran to watch two cosplayers acting out a scene from *The Blasphemers'* season one finale.

"Thanks for playing along with her."

"It was my pleasure. I love to see kids at conventions. All that wonder and excitement." Ella considered asking the woman if the two of them wanted to walk around with her.

"Well, she watches with her dad more than she watches with me, but we enjoy going to conventions together. Cali has been to over twenty of them already."

Ella's gaydar silenced, and this was the way it went for the firefighter. Cute kid dragging around a gorgeous mom, and down the hall there's a dad. "Family fun. That's so great."

"It really is, and thanks again. I shouldn't let her get too far ahead."

Ella watched her walk away and turned in the opposite direction, heading toward the vendor hall to take advantage of the VIP early entry. The exchange had been moments from being awkward, and she thanked the universe for the reprieve.

The door to the vendor hall opened, and one by one, the VIP badges passed under the scanner and attendees, costumed or not, entered. Ella was on the prowl for the signature blaze-orange flaming stripe the Arsonist artwork had, and she was not disappointed. This new show overwhelmed the fantasy science fiction world and, from the appearance of the vendor hall, the art world, too.

Ella spent a few minutes at the first row of tables, passing the vendors that didn't carry her style of art. She loved black and white charcoal sketches but her favorite were the watercolor ink and pen style. There was plenty of talent at this year's event, but one table down aisle C grabbed her attention.

"Your stuff is really nice," Ella said, and she caught a not-so-subtle crinkle in the vendor's nose and a tight flex of their shoulders. She had no talent with a pen or pencil, or any other art medium, so this was her chance to buy from the people that did.

"Thanks, your cosplay is nice too." The woman swished her hair to the side, and Ella noticed that the green streaks highlighted the grey in her eyes.

Ella flipped through the postcard sized pieces. "Your Bruiser is about the best I've seen so far."

The compliment made the artist smile, and she looked closer at Ella. "He was my favorite."

"Not the Arsonist, though? I don't see much artwork except for this one, and it's a bit gruesome." The sketch was black and white line art, with only the color red spurting from the wounds peppered over the character's shoulders. There wasn't a single episode in season one or two that put the Arsonist in line with a bullet. Ella pulled it aside to purchase it.

"I'm not a fan."

That much was obvious, and it got Ella's attention. "How can you not be a fan? She helped catch the Finisher at the end of season one. And she towed that trailer full of liquid filament gas away from the housing colony just in time to save the entire district in episode seven of season two." Ella's hands waved as she explained with unrestrained enthusiasm.

"I found the character beyond redemption after she killed the Bruiser in season one."

"After what?" Ella paused to consider the words she just heard. "Wait, what?"

"When she threw that match." Morgan explained. "I watched the flames spread around the hotel room the Bruiser was in. I loved the Bruiser, and that's just that. I hate when shows pretend to be queer friendly and then kill off those same characters."

"You didn't watch season two at all, did you?"

Morgan shook her head. "Nope, the Arsonist killed it for me." She waved her finger up and down to point at Ella's ensemble. "Although your cosplay is probably the best I've seen."

"What's your name, if I might ask?"

Morgan's cheek raised with a smirking half grin. "I guess you might, and you will, and it's Morgan. Why?"

"Well, Morgan." Ella hooked her gloved hands on her hips and kicked her foot forward in the character's most patronizing signature stance. She grumbled in her best Arsonist voice. "If you'd watched just one episode of season two, you would know that the Arsonist lit the fire that burned down the *Finisher's* lair and that Bruiser wasn't anywhere near that blaze and when the team returned to their secret headquarters at the Florist's, the Arsonist got a new scarf crocheted by the Bruiser to celebrate the big win." Ella made the letter *W* with her gloved hands before crossing her arms in front of her chest, a move that was tight and squeaky from the oversized rubber shoulders on her costume's sleeve.

Morgan's cheeks turned red. "Are you serious?"

"How can you be a fan? How can you make fan art and not know this?" Ella felt her mask slip on her cheek. The discussion was causing her forehead to sweat, so she tugged the drawstring over her ear.

"Like I said. I stopped watching."

"Did you stop watching everything? Because the finale of season two had that group shot that was all over the internet." She opened the pouch on her belt to take out a ten-dollar bill.

"I'm too busy for that."

"You're too busy for the internet?" Ella felt heat rising to her cheeks. This artist was too much. How could anyone hate her favorite character?

"I'm not too busy for the internet, jeez. I'm just too busy for all the fangirling and all of that."

Ella was ready to move on from the table but threw out one more question. "You don't like androgynous women?"

"I like all kinds of people, especially women. I just don't like the one that murdered my favorite character." Morgan took the money, tucked the artwork into a paper bag, and handed it to Ella. When she was finished, she crossed her arms with a level of defensiveness to match the person in front of her.

Ella kicked the heels of her costumed boots, mimicking the Arsonist's exit maneuver. "You should watch the next season." She waved her hand in the air, holding tight to the piece of artwork, turned in her best military style, and walked away. "Kids are so much easier." She said under her breath as she moved on toward the creators in row D.

She watched the Arsonist cosplayer march away from her booth, taking a long moment to admire with an artist's eye the attention to detail that went into the backside of the costume. The oversized seams of the suspender straps highlighted the broad shoulders of the person beneath the costume. Female or male, Morgan was definitely curious, and from the tone of their banter, slightly aroused.

"You really haven't watched season two?" the vendor beside Morgan asked as she clipped the loose threads from the edge of a leather harness. She was making custom fit holsters. "I'm Kelsey, by the way." She launched forward with enthusiasm.

"Hi." Morgan reached over the table display to shake her hand. "I'm Morgan, and that's right. I haven't watched the second season, and I don't plan on watching the third."

"But you do fan art?" There was a tone of accusation in Kelsey's question as she smeared a line of sealant on the freshly cut edge of leather.

"That's because I'm a fan." Her arms crossed, and her hip hitched as she locked into a serious and defensive posture.

"You're a fan of the Bruiser and not a fan of the Arsonist." She pointed back and forth between the pieces of artwork.

"Yep, but I do other art, too. I just didn't bring a bunch for this show." Morgan opened the portfolio she kept under the table. "I do art for *Fairyfires*." She turned the pages one by one. "*The Worst of Them*. Which was one of my first fan art collections." The book held a combination of black and white and color prints of work from the last ten years.

Kelsey took the leather bound portfolio and fanned through. Her hands stopped, and she held the book up at Morgan. "You made character cards for the *Brodies*!"

Morgan smiled. "That was a commission. Not my favorite show, but I got paid so, yep."

"Have you made cards for *Blasphemers*?"

Morgan took the book as Kelsey passed it back. "No, I didn't like how they killed off Bruiser, so I kinda stuck with season one pieces."

"He isn't dead, you know." Kelsey's expression was a deep dimpled smirk.

"So I've learned." She thought about the costumed patron and who might be under all of that silicone and fabric.

"There's a season three watch party tonight. They're showing the premiere episode that won't air until next year. You should come and check it out." Kelsey proposed.

"Are you asking me to go with you?"

Kelsey shook her head. "Nah, I'm just saying you should give it a chance. From the looks of it, the Arsonist kicks some ass in the season opener promotional video." She reached into her pocket and turned on the screen of her phone. In a quick second she was playing the two-minute trailer for season three of *The Blasphemers*.

Morgan grinned as the Bruiser rolled yarn into a ball while he yelled at the Florist. "They changed his beard. He looks so cute." She admired the actor's presence on the screen. "Maybe I will check it out."

"You should. And maybe that hot-headed cosplayer will be there too."

Morgan shrugged. "Maybe, but there's no way I could hang out with the enemy."

"So not the enemy." Kelsey turned away to help a customer, and they left Morgan wondering.

CHAPTER 4

"On or off?" she asked herself as she walked to her car. "What would the Arsonist do?"

Ella pulled at the loops on her gloves to take them off. *The Blasphemers* season three world premiere screening started in a half hour and she wondered if wearing the costume would get in the way. Her six foot tall frame, with almost eight inches of added headpiece helmet height, could block the view of everyone behind her. Her VIP pass came with reserved seating in the theater's front, and there was no way to be six feet tall and discreetly front and center.

"Off," she said to herself as she unclipped the shoulder of her costume pants. Ella folded the pieces one by one, as if handling a newborn child. Her fingers hooked under the lid, once and then a second time to confirm the costume was secured in the trunk of her car. The contest was tomorrow, and after hours walking around the venue, she was pleased that many *Blasphemer* fans had given her a solid, "Yeah dude!" She felt like a shoo-in for top prize.

Ella felt more comfortable in costume at conventions. Her enthusiasm for deconstructing on-screen design had grown each year as her skills with needle and thread improved. Hot glue, too, but she used that less and less when bits began falling off midday. She stacked her vacation time, holding every day so she could drive Charlene to accessible conventions. The Blacktree Comic Palooza convention was her first VIP experience, and aside from the confrontation with that artist earlier in the day, she'd had the best time, taking pictures and gaining attention for months of hard work on her cosplay ensemble.

Ella slid her faded jeans over the spandex she wore with her costume, checked her pockets, and looped her badge over her head. Premiere time was less than fifteen minutes away. She needed to pick up the pace.

~~~~~~~~~~

"Pass please?" The volunteer held a hand up for Ella to stop, scanner at the ready.

"It's right here." She looked down at her chest and felt for the lanyard that should be around her neck. "I know I put it back on."

The volunteer shook their head, and with a monotone voice that would put anyone to sleep, they said, "Step to the side and find your photo ID please." It was clear to Ella that this person scanning VIP badges was unamused by her inability to keep track of a laminated card, punched with a hole so that con-goers could wear it and *not* lose it. The volunteer whose badge read "Sam, she/her," pushed the button on her radio to call for an ID check.

"I went to take off my costume. I know I put it around my neck." Although it should have been a necklace, she patted
~~~~~~~~~~

her front and back pockets. She traveled lightly, always a small card wallet in her front pocket and a phone in her back. Nothing to go ding in a scanner and nothing to accidentally leave behind.

"Just stand over there." Sam pointed to where five people stood in an embarrassed cluster. Their pocket pats were a clear sign that each was experiencing the same problem as Ella. Time ticked, minute by minute, and she feared missing one of the reasons she'd gone to her car to change in the first place.

"Hey," Ella said as she joined the group. "I guess we all can't be trusted as VIPs, huh?"

Three of the people laughed, and one was too upset to care about anything but getting inside. The wait seemed to drag on, but it was less than five minutes before a staff member appeared with a tablet, hand scanner, and a neck full of VIP lanyards.

"Okay, say nothing." She held up a finger to silence any chance for questions. "I just want to see hands. Which of you are going inside to attend the premiere screening?" Her badge read "Mel, she/her," and she wasn't wasting words. Ella's hand popped up with two others. "Okay, you three are first, since it's about to start. IDs, please?"

Mel was quick, and one by one she compared names to the VIP list on her frighteningly dim tablet. She gave each of the attendees a new lanyard, along with a warning. "One and done for the five of you; you lose it again, and you'll have to purchase a day pass."

Ella stuck her head through the previous year's bright orange lanyard with a current VIP badge on the end. Nothing says *I lost my badge* like a glowing ribbon from last year around your neck.

"Also, don't try to scan the lost badge if you find it. Theft of service is a felony because of the VIP value. If you find it, throw it away, and make sure you've got your ID for the rest of the con."

Ella felt scolded and embarrassed on a fifth-grade level as she entered the end of the VIP line. "Thanks, Sam," she said as the scanner beeped and she entered the theater.

The convention reserved the first three rows for VIP guests, and Ella took one of the least desired seats off to the side. As one of the last to enter, it wasn't a great screen angle, but it was better than being all the way in the back.

"This is going to be so good." She rubbed her hands across the length of her thighs, vibing on the nervous energy in the room.

"I know." The person beside her was fidgeting. "That season finale, though." They held their hands up beside their head to mimic an explosion. "Mind blown, pow!"

"Crazy, right?" Ella smiled.

Everyone in the theater was a fan of the show, some even more than she was. As she admired so many in fan shirts and cosplay outfits, she realized that somewhere in this crowd sat her competition. Tomorrow she'd give it her all at the costume event.

"Who is your favorite?" the person next to her asked. "The Bruiser? No, the Specialist. You look like you're into the brainy type."

Ella rolled her forearm over and pulled the band of her watch up to reveal the flamethrower logo tattooed there. She thought about the artist who drew it. How her tongue jetted out from the corner of her mouth as she sketched the three-toned flames. Yeah, she loved the tattoo.

"Arsonist, yeah, that's fucking cool." The person scrunched the sleeve to their shoulder to reveal the outline of a boxing glove hitting a brick wall.

"Bruiser." Ella shook her head. "You've watched all the episodes, so you're aware the Arsonist didn't murder the Bruiser, right?"

The person's brow scrunched into the most sour expression. "Hell yeah. Who would think that?"

"Ah, nothing. Just a vendor I met today. She's an excellent artist. Check out her stuff because she's a ridiculous season one Bruiser superfan."

"Cool, thanks." They held a hand out. "I'm Jackson, by the way. Jack for short." He smiled, and Ella shook his hand.

"Ella, Nice to meet you."

"Yeah, so you're into fire?" he asked. It was clear by the way he tipped his shoulders and swiped his untamed hair that he was working hard to be cool.

"I guess I'm more into putting them out, but I like the way she kicks ass with a flamethrower."

"Put them out?" He thought about Ella's answer. "You a fireman?"

She rolled her eyes internally. Did she look like a man? Maybe it was the long curly hair. Or the size C bra cup. Maybe it was the she/her pronouns, but he obviously didn't see that. Her badge was new, and she hadn't written her name and pronouns on it yet. Clearly in her tight fitting Blasphemers t-shirt she had to be a fire*man*.

"Yeah, I'm a firefighter."

"That's pretty cool." He fidgeted with the zipper on his hip bag before sharing. "I drive a bus for the city of Blacktree. I have one of the West side routes."

"That's a big rig. A lot like our ladder trucks."

"With less fire and not many emergencies." He laughed at his own joke. "But I get my fair share of drama."

"Emergencies and drama are my life."

"You on socials?" He held up his phone.

Ella nodded her head and wiggled hers from her back pocket. This was where the conversation changed. It almost always did. "Here." She held up the code for him to scan, and she watched as her life in images rolled one by one at the tip of his finger.

"No shit!" He looked down at his phone and back up at her. "Are you really @Cinder_ellaE?"

"That's me." She shoved her phone back into her pocket and watched Jack scroll through her page.

After a few minutes of pictures, videos, and promotions, in his eyes, they were now best buds. "I saw this one." He showed the picture of Ella dressed in her Santa suit for the month of December last year. "I bought the calendar for my sister." He leaned closer and added with a whisper. "She's gay, too."

"Thanks for the support." She whispered back a little too loudly to be considered a whisper. "I'm lucky enough that I'll be in it again this year." *Lucky enough*, she thought. More like forced to dress in the most ridiculous outfit possible, but at least she got June, and there would be a reason for her to wear a crop top.

"December again?"

The lights in the theater dimmed, and Ella whispered. "New year, new month."

"My sister will be happy to hear that."

A voice came over the intercom. "Sit back and shut your blasphemous mouths! Episode one of season three is here." The room erupted with piercing whistles and screams as a rainbow countdown clock appeared on the wall.

Ella didn't say another word as the Arsonist's flamethrower scribbled the charred title of the show on a brick wall.

"That was a great season premiere," Kelsey said as they exited the theater, side by side and a bit closer than Morgan liked.

It was a bizarre extension of theater magic, this bond created by fans in a fandom, but Kelsey, although cute and positive, just wasn't her type.

"Some of it didn't make sense," she said as she adjusted the vendor lanyard around her neck.

She and Kelsey entered the theater just as the countdown clock began and had to stand for the entire 53 minutes along the back wall. Her legs would be sore later. They weren't alone as the room was packed with fans eager to see what the new season had in store. The teaser at the end was thirty seconds long and revealed cuts and clips of the next fifteen episodes. No context, no timeline, just ridiculous bits of what was to come and the special effects and costuming changes you have when a show gets a bigger budget.

"You should watch season two," Kelsey suggested as she turned toward the building exit. "Are you staying for the mixer tonight?"

"I'm planning to stay late tomorrow, so I'm heading home."

"It's great to be local, isn't it?"

Morgan nodded. "I wish this convention was here every year. I had a super successful day." She adjusted the bag on her shoulder to balance the fatigue in her legs. Long days away from the shop were hard on her.

"Tomorrow, with a full day of fandom, it'll be even bigger and better."

Kelsey waved as she walked to the exit door. Morgan wanted to make one last check on her table, inventory her supplies, and grab the bank deposit bag before heading to the vendor lot. She wasn't paying attention to the crowd as she turned toward the long hallway.

"Did you enjoy the season premiere?" The question and tone of voice demanded attention, and Morgan was curious. She didn't recognize the voice, and when she turned around, it surprised her to see a tall dark-haired woman with cloudy brown eyes looking at her.

"I suppose. It was good."

"Good?" The woman smiled knowingly, but what she knew, Morgan wasn't sure.

"I was a little bit lost," Morgan admitted. She had no idea why she was talking to this stranger.

"Ah, you're not a fan of the show?"

"I am. I just…it's a little complicated." She turned to walk to the vendor hall.

"You're a vendor?" Morgan's body language changed as this stranger invited her to talk about her passion. She lived for art.

"I am. I do fan art and some other things. I have a studio in town."

"Another local, that's so great." The woman adjusted the lanyard that was bouncing against her chest.

"You too? Are you a vendor? I don't remember seeing you." The pace of their steps slowed as they approached a restricted area.

"Nope, not a vendor. I work in emergency services." The woman smiled. "I'm just here as a fan."

Morgan stopped to do a quick scan of her new companion, really taking the woman in from head to toe. Broad shoulders, tight biceps and thin ripped forearms. This person definitely made a living with her body. "Are you on the volunteer team for first aid?"

"Oh," she said, as if she'd never considered that before. "That's a good idea for next year, but no."

"Are you going to make me keep guessing?" Morgan gently punched the woman's arm and was surprised to feel her body was as hard as it looked. She was trying to see the front of this stranger's badge where the name and pronouns would be on display.

Ella caught the casual glance. "My name's Ella, in case you were wondering." She flipped her badge around, forgetting that she hadn't written her name on the replacement yet.

"Morgan." Her hand flicked out to offer a shake.

"It's very nice to meet you, Morgan–the artist and not quite a fan."

The comment made them both laugh, although it was an awkward and nervous exchange.

"I'm a fan. It's just that I had a weird thing with a guest today."

"Super fan?" Ella asked.

"It's a very long story, but yes. I think they were a super fan of the Arsonist." Morgan slowed her pace. She liked the conversation with this stranger and didn't want it to end.

"You're not a fan of the Arsonist?" But there was a look in Ella's eyes that Morgan couldn't quite read.

"That's the long story part." Morgan shrugged, her hand fiddling with the badge and lanyard, wanting to go but also curious enough to stay.

Ella lingered as Morgan stopped in front of the vendor hall. "Would you like to have a drink? Maybe share that long story?"

Morgan displayed her badge to the security volunteer at the door. "If you can wait? I think I'd like that."

"Oh, I can wait." Ella smiled broadly, then rested against the wall, looking like she was about to strike up a conversation with the security guard.

Morgan walked to her table, made a quick count of sales to get a rough number in her head, and tucked the cash pouch into the bag on her shoulder. She knew she was rushing, but she was certainly curious about this new person. She didn't run. Her legs were too tired for that, but she hurried to return and was delighted to find the woman was exactly where she'd left her.

"Do you want to go to the bar here?" Morgan asked as they stood beside the closing door.

"We could, or I know a place around the corner. It won't be too loud to talk."

Morgan thought about the area. As a local, she could only come up with one place. "Are you thinking about the Sage Lounge?"

"You know it?" Ella asked as she and Morgan walked side by side toward the convention center lobby.

"I go there a lot," Morgan said. "Probably more than I should. It's a great place to sketch and work without many outrageous distractions."

"I'm not an artist, but I appreciate the environment, and the staff are rock stars. Would you like to go there?" Ella asked, as she held the door open.

"Yes, that'd be great. Kinda perfect, really."

The sidewalk was congested with convention goers, some costumed and some not, but most had badges bouncing in front of their bodies. Morgan knew she and Ella had *The Blasphemers* in common, but she also wanted to get to know this curious woman a little better.

"So, you said emergency services. What do you do exactly?"

Ella's hands were in her pockets. She flexed her shoulders as she said, "I'm a firefighter."

Morgan stopped walking, taken aback by the woman's profession. She couldn't be with a firefighter, could she? She knew about fire firsthand and could only imagine the dangers Ella must face. But it was only a few drinks. *Just drinks,* she thought.

"So you're a firefighter here in the city?"

Ella nodded. "Station eight eighteen."

"Huh." Morgan made the sound as she skipped to catch up with Ella's longer strides.

"What does 'huh' mean?"

Morgan didn't answer. She just looked up and down at Ella, contemplating how to explain her reaction. The woman looked less like a firefighter and more like a bodybuilder or trainer. When did she find time to put out fires?

"You're trying to understand how someone who fights fires can obsess over a TV character that starts them?"

Morgan smiled. "Well, there is that, but no. I was honestly just surprised that's what you do. I didn't see you handling hoses and stuff like that."

Ella laughed at that. "We handle many things." She must've realized her pace was faster than Morgan's shorter legs because she slowed her stride almost to a standstill. "So you thought my job was what?"

The artist smiled and glanced obviously at Ella's body, "Personal trainer or fitness nut. Maybe a model."

"Hmm, well, I work out for the job, but I'm not a fitness 'nut.'" She made little quotation marks in the air. "I don't train anyone but myself, and I might have modeled once or twice but not by choice."

Morgan's eyebrow raised, wondering what that could mean. "Not by choice? How's that work?"

"It was a fundraising thing." She stopped as a group of people pushed them to the edge of the sidewalk. Ella's hand came up to catch Morgan, who was inches from tripping off the sidewalk's curb.

"Thanks," Morgan said, and they continued down the street. "So with the modeling and fitness, why are you a firefighter?"

Ella's mouth opened and closed, clearly wanting to give a cheeky answer, but she said, "That's probably just as long of a story as you have to share about *The Blasphemers*."

They turned the corner and a few minutes later they were at the entrance to the Sage Lounge. Ella reached for the handle, but Morgan stepped in first.

"My turn," she said and held the door open for the nearly six foot tall woman.

"Thank you."

"You're welcome." Morgan said, just as an enthusiastic greeting came from behind the host stand.

"Cinder-Ella, baby girl, how are you?" The host grinned. He stood just above Ella, a thick man with a dark head shaved clean and a button-up shirt that looked like it just came from a starch factory.

"Hey, Marsh, you sugar plum," she said just before the solid arms came around to hug her.

"Missed you at the gym today," he said, tugging the lanyard around her neck. "Ooh, your con was this weekend. I forgot. How'd it go?"

"Pretty good. Did you hit a personal goal without me at the gym?" she asked.

The man raised a flexed bicep. His arm was the size of Morgan's thigh.

"Never, not without my Cinder-Ella to count those reps."

"Put the guns away. You'll get me excited." Ella joked. "So, Marshy plum, you got a table for me and my new friend, Mor—?" Her question was cut off as the host scooped Morgan up in his arms.

"Crumbly!" He squeezed her tight before setting her to the floor like a porcelain doll.

"Crumbly?" Ella repeated, a questioning eyebrow raised .

"She's my Crumbly." He hooked his finger into the loop of Morgan's shoulder bag. "You know, artists and pencils and erasers make crumbs all over the table. Crumbly!" The explanation was crystal clear to Morgan and Marsh, but Ella seemed clueless. Morgan figured she must really not know about art and the crumbs left behind by their creators. "You ladies know each other?" Marsh waved a finger between the two.

"We just met." They said almost at the same time.

"It's a first date with two of my favorites." He pointed at the rack on the wall. "Menus? Or just your regular drinks?"

"I think we're just having drinks," Morgan said, looking at Ella for confirmation.

"Yep, just drinks. If you have a quiet spot for us, that would be great."

"Coming right up." He stepped around them toward the spiral stairs leading to the second story. "You okay on the stairs tonight, Crumbs?"

"A-okay today, Marshy plum." She would ask him about the delicious nickname at a later time. And also about this intriguing woman they had in common.

Marsh led them up the steps to the quietest spot in the lounge. He pulled out a chair for Morgan, but before he could help Ella, she sat on the opposite side. "Your first round is on me. I'll bring up your regular drinks in a minute." He walked away and came back a few seconds later with a huge bowl of pretzels.

"How do you know Marsh?" Morgan asked as she popped a pretzel in her mouth.

Ella laughed. "We work out at the same gym."

"He power lifts. Do you do that, too?"

"I lift with him, but I'm not as serious as he is."

"Not serious, really?" The deliberate glance at Ella's body didn't go unnoticed.

"People expect a lot in an emergency. I just want to deliver."

"That's admirable." Morgan leaned closer, interested in this firefighting fangirl. "It's a small world that we both know Marsh. What's the whole Cinder-Ella thing? You got a glass slipper?"

Ella didn't laugh at the joke. "It's a high school thing and so embarrassing after nearly fifteen years." She shook her head as she explained. "I was really good at putting out campfires, and since my name is Ella, the joke became a screwed up nickname. Sometimes those last forever, and as much as you'd like them to, they just never go away. So now I embrace it."

"That's cute that you were putting out fires as a teenager."

"Didn't make me very popular with a bunch of drunk teenagers freezing their asses off at the bonfires, though."

"No!" Morgan realized the teenagers were trying to light fires and covered her mouth to hide the laugh. "That's terrible."

"Yeah." Ella's arms raised to rest on the table. "How about you tell me about Crumbly?"

Morgan leaned back in her chair and rolled the hem of her shirt between her fingers. "I come in here to work. If I'm having a hard day at the office, I break out the pencils."

"The office?" Ella raised a questioning eyebrow.

"I have a gallery about six blocks from here."

Ella smiled. "That's so great that you sell your work out of a gallery."

"Yep. So on pencil days, I might draw a bunch of reference lines, and if I have to clean them up, I make crumbs with my eraser."

"I had no idea."

Morgan shrugged her shoulders. "Why would you? Most people don't, but I try to make polite messes when I'm creating art in public, so by the time I'm finished, I have a little pile of eraser crumbs on a napkin. Marsh teased me after the third time I came in, and it just kind of stuck."

"That's so much better than Cinder."

"Maybe, but they both seem pretty similar."

A server delivered their drinks to the table. Morgan knew him, and from the smile Ella gave him, she must've too. "Hello, I didn't realize you were friends."

"We just met," they said at the same time. Short laughs turned into awkward silence.

Ella picked up her seltzer and twirled the stir stick a few times before taking a drink.

"You're a firefighter," Morgan said after the server had left. "How did that happen?"

Ella smiled and went into the long story about watching documentaries and obsessing about forest fires and how much she wanted to become a park ranger to help prevent them. It turned out that she was better suited for emergency services that didn't keep her isolated and covering miles of territory alone. Morgan laughed at all the silly jokes, and before long, it was after midnight. Their small bowl of pretzels was gone, but neither of them were ready to end the evening.

"It's getting a little late," Ella said and pulled her wallet from the deep front pocket of her pants.

"I didn't even realize." Morgan rolled her wrist to check her watch. "You're very good at this." She twirled her finger to point at the empty glasses and bowl of pretzels.

"Does that mean we can do it again?" Ella stood and put the cash on the table.

"I'd like that."

~~~~~~~~~~

"What?" Beatrice's grumbling, half awake sounds made Morgan smile over the phone. It was clear that her best friend was sleeping, but Morgan had to tell her all about the hot firefighter.

"I kinda had a date."

She heard a bed creaking. Beatrice must have jolted up like a pastry in a toaster at the news. "NO WAY!"

"Way, and she was hot. Not like the chick at the ticket counter at the theater hot. Like firefighter hot." It all spilled out of her without pause, and she gulped for air as she waited for a response.

"A real firefighter? Or one of those cosplayer fire creatures you're always bitching about drawing?" Her voice was
~~~~~~~~~~

fuzzy and drawn, definitely not one hundred percent invested in the conversation.

"Oh no, she's real. I touched her." Morgan didn't even try to hide the smile on her face.

"Wait, what?" Beatrice sounded more awake now. "You slept with her?"

"Whoa, slow your ride, cowgirl." Morgan drove the few blocks home, put the truck in park, and relaxed back into her seat to finish the call. "We sat at the Sage and talked."

"You said there was touching." There was a pause, then Beatrice said, "You know it's one o'clock in the morning."

"Yeah, sorry. The only touching was all very innocent. And did I tell you about her muscles?"

"You said hot, and it kinda sounded like there were exclamation marks at the end of it."

Morgan thought about their parting moment, always awkward on a first *kinda* date, if that's what it was. She wanted to kiss her, but she also didn't want to send a message that it would go any farther. But she thought, just from the way Ella carried herself, that she'd been kissed many times before.

"Did you?"

Morgan realized she'd gotten lost in thought and hadn't been listening. "Sorry, did I what?"

"Did you get a picture of her?"

Morgan grabbed her sling bag and threw it over her shoulder. "I didn't. That would have been weird."

"Are you going to see her again?"

Morgan thought about the question. They'd exchanged numbers, and she liked the woman. "I sure hope so."

CHAPTER 5

"Nah, man," Ella said as she sandwiched her phone between her ear and her shoulder. This was the balancing act of a late night and early rising. "I didn't get home until after midnight."

She wasn't upset about the late night walk to the car or the short drive home in the dark. The conversation with Morgan excited her, and although she needed to come clean about their cosplay encounter, she thought the petite woman with grey eyes and green tipped hair might be worth getting to know.

"Hot chick or cosplay party?" Lester joked.

"Maybe it was both. Did you ever consider that?" She wiggled into her costume pants.

"Not with you and that show obsession." She could hear him puttering around his kitchen. Knowing him, he was probably on his second or third cup of coffee. "Did you win?"

She switched to speaker and laid the phone in her trunk. "I don't know yet. The contest starts in about..." She stopped to look at her watch. "Shit, man, ten minutes. I gotta go." She ended the call just as Lester started asking about the hot chick. Ella pinned the number twenty-seven to the hip of her costume pants. With her entry form submitted for the cosplay contest, all she had to do was be there when they called her number. "You've got this," she said to herself as she checked for the third time that her VIP badge was hanging around her neck. She looked at her reflection in Charlene's side mirror. "You've totally got this."

Ella was fit. She worked out five days a week, but the costume was nothing like her turn-out gear, and it was a good thing that she could enter the venue through the VIP entrance or she would have missed the costume contest. Her number was called just after entering the hall.

The costumes on stage were a combination of thrift store garb, detailed reproductions, and everything in between. The event staff organized the cosplayers by show and character, and although there were twelve other Arsonists, Ella's received the loudest and most enthusiastic reception.

"The Blacktree Comic Palooza convention would like to thank all eighty-nine participants in this year's cosplay contest. The most ever!" The announcer cleared her throat as she looked offstage, waiting for confirmation that they tallied the votes. "And it looks like we have winners." A judge walked out carrying an official Blacktree Comic Palooza convention clipboard. "If I may." She took the list from the judge. "There is absolutely a clear winner. Oooh and it looks like they're a first time participant." She clapped awkwardly, crashing the clipboard against the microphone.

Ella looked at the cosplayers beside her. *The Blasphemers* had a definite following and made up more than half of the entries. As she eyed the costumes side by side, she thought the attention to detail paid to the Specialist costume standing three people away from her was her real competition.

The Specialist was the show's tech and weapons guru, and the lights and digital FX on this costume blew Ella's thumb flame out of the water. If she wasn't going to win, she wanted this cosplayer to take the top prize.

More than being the winner at the top, Ella wanted that prize, which was a VIP pass to next year's event. Another con that was just across the state line a few hours away. And with a prize value of over six hundred dollars, it might make it affordable for her to attend the next traveling event. She was so lost in thought that she didn't hear her name called the first time.

"Are you El Eastern?" The cosplayer elbowed Ella.

"One more time, the top prize goes to our Blasphemous Arsonist, El Eastern."

The crowd was out of their seats, screaming and cheering for Ella. She almost didn't care that they'd mispronounced her name. Her arm went up as she performed her very best prize winning wave.

"Our winner, everyone." The announcer grabbed Ella's gloved hand and shook it over their heads like a champion boxer.

She was definitely the crowd favorite, and Ella didn't even mind when they pinned the gaudy oversized Champion ribbon on her costume's suspenders.

"Thank you," Ella said in her most grumbled and gravely imitation of the Arsonist. "Everyone up here is a winner, though. We all know how many hours were spent creating these costumes, so let's cheer for everyone."

The crowd went wild, screaming and whistling until convention volunteers escorted the participants from the stage.

"This is so amazing," Ella said to no one in particular. She was still awed at having won.

She stopped offstage to take a selfie and record the moment to post later on social media. Celebration was in her future. After the excitement of drinks with Morgan and today's win, she thought the day was perfect. That is, until she really thought about last night and Morgan and having to come clean about who she was and how much she knew about the artist. *It wasn't deception, was it?* she thought to herself. Perhaps it was, and with that, she decided to avoid the vendor hall and get in line for her meet and greet session with the one and only original Arsonist, Dracea Barnes. The woman had it all: great looks, amazing physical abilities, and the ultimate action hero role. To say Ella idolized her was a mild assessment.

She checked her watch, noticing she had just enough time to grab a quick cup of coffee to take to the meet and greet session. The line outside the hotel shop was long, and she hoped it would move fast enough to satisfy her need for caffeine. She smiled when she heard the voice behind her; the sound was welcome until she remembered she was in costume.

"I guess congratulations are in order," Morgan said, pointing at the gaudy ribbon as she leaned forward, out of the way of the customers standing between them.

Ella put on her best grumbly Arsonist voice. "Uh, thanks."

"The crowd loved you." Morgan held up her phone to play the recorded announcement that was already receiving viewer hits and likes.

"The costume is fucking unreal, man," the person standing between them added.

"Yeah, I put a lot of hours in. I'm thrilled for the win."

"And VIP for next year? That's a bomb-rocket prize, dude." Their fist came up for a knuckle bump, and Ella was happy to take part as long as it kept Morgan from discovering her true identity.

The line continued to advance and within minutes Ella was ordering a super sized cup of hot, black caffeine.

"That's a lot of coffee," Morgan said, mostly to herself.

"Late night and early morning," Ella replied as she paid and collected her drink. Before Morgan could say another word, Ella disappeared into the crowd.

She made it to the meet and greet with minutes to spare, which left no time for her to remove the helmet or heavy components of her costume. From the moment she walked into the room, she could feel Dracea Barnes' eyes on her. It was like the other people in the room were invisible to her. The actor stood up and held out her hand for Ella to shake.

"I was hoping I would see you before they shuffle me out today." Dracea leaned back to inspect the costume from head to toe. "You're a real artist." She released Ella, and the volunteer escort helped her to the assigned seat.

"Thanks."

Ella sat down, and because coffee was impossible to drink through the helmet, she unsnapped the chin strap and placed it on the floor beside her. For the next thirty minutes, the room buzzed with questions about the show, Dracea's career, and the audition process for *The Blasphemers*. Ella was captivated. She wouldn't say she was star struck, more delighted to discover that the actor was as pleasant in real life as she'd always believed.

"Wow, you have all been so wonderful!" Dracea said as she stood. "Can we do a group shot for my social media?" she asked the volunteer escort.

"It's your call," they said. "You're the boss in here."

"Oh, I like that!" She waved everyone together. Ella was quick to put her headpiece back on for the photos. "Staying in character. That's very admirable," Dracea joked as she positioned herself beside Ella.

"I don't want to blow my secret identity," Ella said with the best Arsonist impersonation.

"Your secret is safe with us." She winked, and Ella had to work twice as hard to digest the way that simple expression made her feel.

"The crowd loved that costume."

Morgan held her phone so that Kelsey could watch the cosplay contest video which had over one hundred thousand views in just a few hours. "Yeah, that's the person who was in here yesterday calling out my hate for the Arsonist."

Kelsey smiled. "Yep, I knew that costume would take the big prize."

"We were in line for coffee just after the contest." Morgan shared. "Seems like a nice person, and I'm going to watch season two so I can understand the rest of season three when it airs."

"They got to you."

"Yeah, maybe a little bit." She smiled, wondering not for the first time who was under all of that silicone and pleather.

"Maybe they're still here?"

Morgan looked at her watch. "The vendor hall closes in a half hour. So they're probably gone forever."

"Are you on social media?" Kelsey asked.

Morgan laughed louder than she should have. "I'm an independent artist and small business owner. Of course, I'm on social media." She opened the app on her phone to reveal her company download code. "Scan away."

Kelsey scanned the code, and the link led to Morgan's website. "Rage Against The System. That's so cool that you own a rage room."

"It helps me cope with the lack of customers in the artist alley of the gift shop."

"You know what would help?" Kelsey asked.

Morgan was curious to know what this leather artist might suggest. A leather section? Adding handmade leather goods to the gift shop? "No, what might help?"

"Getting the Arsonist inside to do a smash video for your social page."

The idea wasn't a terrible one, Morgan thought. "I wonder how I can find them?" she whispered under her breath.

"Maybe a bit of investigative work?" Kelsey said as she began to cover her displays for the night. "Open the convention's social media site and find them. They have to be there after today."

~~~~~~~~~~

Morgan spent more than a half hour walking the convention hall in search of a very specific Arsonist. Their paths didn't cross again, and although she was certain she could locate them through social media, the idea felt a bit like stalking. Her drive home was short and when she passed the Sage Lounge, her thoughts drifted to the night before and her evening with the cutest firefighter in the city. She parked the truck, but before she went into her loft apartment she sent a quick text message to her new friend.

Morgan: *I didn't see you around the convention today. Did you have a good time?*

A few seconds passed, and she watched the typing dots appear.

Ella: *Great day at the con. Best day ever. Sorry I was too busy to come see you.*

Morgan: *Will I see you at the con tomorrow?*

Ella: *Sorry, no. I'm back at the station tomorrow. Called in to cover a shift. Waste of a VIP day.*
~~~~~~~~~~

Morgan's sigh was loud as she slammed the door of the truck. "Stupid, I should have stayed longer to find her," she said to herself as she walked to her apartment.

Ella: *Coffee some time?*
Morgan: *I'd really like that.*
Ella: *My next day off is Tuesday.*
Morgan: *I'm in. My shop opens at noon. How about 9 am at the Sage?*
Ella: *I'll be there.*

Morgan stared at the screen on her phone, wishing she had more to say, but texting was so impersonal, and she really liked Ella. She wanted to see her face and watch her expressions change when they shared their conversation. *I can wait until Tuesday, she thought. It's only a few days.*

CHAPTER 6

"Fuck this!" Her body trembled, almost disconnected, but somehow tied to the tragedy. Her gloves were at her feet and blood caked in droplets peppered the dirt beside them. Ella threw the wrench, and it bounced off the grass, landing in a pile of rocks. She was standing beside the wreckage, a mangled and unidentifiable side impacted minivan. The blood-stained pink princess blanket tangled in the belt behind the driver's seat, a reminder of who pays when seatbelts aren't worn.

"We did all that we could, Cind—Eastman." Lester put a hand on her shoulder, but she didn't want comfort. She wanted to run time in reverse to prevent this accident from ever happening.

"Kids though, man. I hate when it's kids."

She dropped to the ground to sit on the curb, her dirt-covered hands rubbing her forehead and cheeks. They'd watched the ambulance pull away from the scene seconds ago with hopeful adults following behind in the police cruiser. They'd learn soon enough that their child didn't survive the collision. The fifteen miles between the accident scene and the hospital were a last hope for her parents, one Ella couldn't bring herself to dash. But the little girl was already gone.

Ella knew what it was like to fall into a nightmare like that and never wake.

"Let's get back to the station."

"I just—"

She stopped, frozen as the blanket caught the ground when the tow truck pitched to drag the car onto the flatbed. There were things you said on the job and things that you would never say.

It was Monday night. She had three hours left in her shift and the next two days off. She knew what she would do: work out, run, workout, and run some more. Nothing ever took away the sound of a parent's screams, the horror of their baby's blood pouring from the car. She could already imagine the anguished cries echoing off the walls of the emergency room. But physical exertion quieted it a little bit.

"I know, Eastman. I know."

It was the last thing Lester said to her that night. The mood in the station house was isolating and as Ella stuffed her shirt into the duffle bag, she thought about coffee in the morning. The feelings, this mood, wouldn't fade. She'd be horrible company, and there was no way she could put all of this on Morgan.

<center>~~~~~~~~~~</center>

Ella: *I hate to do this, but I can't make it this morning. Something came up.*

Morgan: *Sorry to hear that. Maybe another time?*

Ella: *Maybe*

Ella stared at the phone. What did she have to offer this sweet woman? Some days, Ella's job was hard on *her*, and the last thing she wanted to do was drag Morgan into it. She rolled over in bed, tugged the covers over her face and tucked the phone under her pillow. Maybe she should keep her world exactly as it was.

~~~~~~~~~~

"Open up Cinder girl!" Lester hammered the door with his fist. He'd phoned and texted Ella all morning, worried about her after last night's call. "I'm not leaving until your face is here in front of me." He hit the door again just as Ella flung it open.

"The fuck, Les!" She wiped her face, half awake but mostly asleep. Her tank top was twisted sideways, revealing half of the swell of her breast. The boxers she'd slept in had tiny seahorses with little fire hoses. Nothing about the way she presented herself showed signs of being out of bed. "You're gonna wake the god damn neighbors, Soot!"

"It's one o'clock in the afternoon. I think your neighbors are at work." He pushed past her to enter the cottage. "You're not sleeping the day away. I'm not going to let you. It's not healthy."

Ella knew what she was doing, and that it was not the solution to the accident response from the night before. She couldn't erase the scene from her thoughts. That little girl tangled in the unfastened seatbelt, surrounded by bits and chunks of shattered glass and shredded steel. No person should ever see that, and if there was any justice, her parents were unconscious long enough not to have that image etched in their memories.

"I just have to work through it," Ella said as she kicked the door closed and walked to the kitchen. "I'll be fine by Friday."

"How's that?" Lester called her bluff and pointed at her current attire. "Laying in bed is not dealing with it."

"Right now, it's the best I've got."
~~~~~~~~~~

Lester walked through the living room and into Ella's bedroom. He opened drawers and grabbed a shirt and pants. "Put this on."

Ella caught the clothes just before they hit the floor. "The hell? I'm not going anywhere, man."

He didn't move to leave her bedroom or turn his back to give her privacy. "Get dressed. We're going to take care of how we feel about last night."

Ella dropped the clothes, crossed her arms, and planted herself to stay.

"Don't be a giant pain in the ass." He raised his voice. "Get dressed."

Her knuckles tightened.

"It's not a request," he told her.

"We're standing in my house and you're pulling rank on me?"

His head shook, more than frustration leading to their next exchange. "I count on you out there, goddamn it! You're an excellent firefighter, Els, and I want to keep it that way."

Ella felt the chest-clenching grip of anger and anxiety. Her job came with unbearable levels of both that she could usually manage at the gym or with a pair of running shoes. "I'm not going to be very good company today."

"That's all right. You're not very good company most days." He punched her shoulder, giving her his best sarcastic grin. "Anyway, we aren't going to do much talking."

Ella was going through the motions as she kicked into her jeans and pulled on the Blacktree Fire Department t-shirt. Her boots were already laced as she pushed her feet in and zipped the sides. Lester was sympathetic, escorting her to his car and driving them a few short miles to a place the two of them could extinguish the flames of grief.

"Rage Against The System?" Ella read the sign above the door. "R.A.T.S. Really?"

"Just trust me. A rage room is exactly what you need today." He opened the passenger door for his friend and coworker.

"Maybe a bat against a wall would be a great idea," she said as she watched the video screen play through clips of previous customer experiences.

"You can hit everything but the walls," the woman said as she walked from the back room.

"That's what we've come to do," Lester said as he threw his arm over Ella's shoulder.

"You're the one-thirty? Feller party plus one?" she asked, laying two pieces of paper on the countertop before either could answer. "Waivers for both of you to sign." She slapped a pen on top of each.

Les slid the page toward Ella. "Great."

The more she watched the video on the tv, the more she liked the idea of smashing things to work out her feelings. "You need an ID…?" Ella asked, tearing her eyes away from the TV screen to read the woman's name tag, then added, "Beatrice?"

"Yes, and are you each other's emergency contact?" She waved her finger back and forth between them.

Lester nodded.

"So if that's the situation, you have to rage in different rooms, just in case." She picked up his form first. "When you called, you said you wanted the heavy package, so we set up some solid choices, more metal and less glass. Is that still okay?" She picked up Ella's form and scrolled through. Ella wasn't sure why, but the woman's eyes went wide.

"I like the idea of hitting something solid." Ella felt a rush of adrenaline snapping her from the haze of emotions. It reminded her of the times Lou had her punch pillows to vent her feelings about the car accident that left her an orphan.

"That's, uh . . . Great," Beatrice said as she looked over her shoulder toward the rooms for raging. "I'm going to take Ella to room number one. I'll come back for you, Lester. You can wander around the gift shop if you like or just have a seat."

She pointed to the row of mismatched plastic and steel chairs; not a single one looked new or comfortable, and after giving a frown that told Ella he'd had the same thought, he went into the gift shop.

He punched a soft blow to Ella's shoulder as he walked by. "Go wild, Cinder."

"Room one." Beatrice opened the door, and Ella stepped inside. "Any tools on that rack are used to strike everything in here, BUT!" She turned to make sure Ella was listening. "Don't smash the rack or the camera." She pointed to the corner where the observation camera hung mounted. "Please put on the jumpsuit." She handed the zip-up one-piece heavy cotton onesie to Ella. "Face mask and gloves. If you're swinging, keep all the protective gear on. Music controls over there." She pointed to the panel built into the wall.

She waited for Ella to cover up, and when she finished, she turned the timer on the wall. "Your guy signed you up for two one-hour sessions. I'll be back when this goes off." She slapped her palm against the meter.

"That's it?" Ella asked as her eyes focused on the aluminum bat resting closest to her.

"The lights will dim, and that's your signal to stop." Without another word, the door closed behind Beatrice.

Ella saw the audio controller on the wall and adjusted the sound to crashing heavy metal, cranked it up, strangle-gripped the bat, and made her first connection with the passenger side door of what looked like a retired street and sanitation pick-up truck.

The sound of crunching metal reminded her of the jaws of life biting through yesterday's car. The minivan had a five star crash test rating except for the side impact adjacent to the unbuckled child. One chance in a million impact, but it never ended well for children in unfastened seats. The bat connected with the tempered glass and it crumbled away in unpredictable clumps.

"Just—a—little—girl."

The bat felt weightless, swing after swing until the door toppled from its perch. Ella adjusted the swing, slamming from over her head and down until the door appeared nothing like it did when the session started.

"Put—on—a—damn seatbelt!" Her scream blended with the squealing guitar of the music.

Morgan came out from the office to find Beatrice standing with a man she didn't recognize. They were both staring up at a monitor.

"She didn't waste any time," Beatrice said as they watched the live video feed.

"Room seven is ready for rage," Morgan told him, then asked Beatrice, "I can set him up if you want?"

"Sure, number one is going." She pointed to the monitor, and Morgan stared for a long moment at the bat swinging hard against the door.

"Wow," was all she could say as she led the man to the opposite side of the building.

"We had a pretty tough call last night," he explained.

"Call?" Morgan looked down at his liability waiver. "Oh, you're both firefighters."

"Yeah, we lost a little kid last night, and she's taking it pretty hard." He pointed his thumb toward the other room.

"I'm sorry about that, but you've definitely come to the right place." She opened the door to Lester's rage space, then gave him the same spiel she was sure Beatrice had given to his friend.

"Thank you," he said, struggling to remember her name. "Sorry I don't remember your—"

"Morgan," she interrupted.

The man–Lester, according to his waiver–gave her an odd look, but didn't say anything.

"Have fun, Lester," she said, then closed the door behind her.

Returning to the office, she watched the monitor on her tablet. "These two are firefighters and they lost a kid last night." She flipped back and forth between the live feeds. "That's so terrible."

Beatrice didn't respond, her eyes glued to the screen in front of her.

"They're both firefighters," Morgan repeated, placing her clipboard on the file rack. "Did you hear me?"

"Did you see what station house?" Beatrice asked.

"I didn't. Why?"

"It's eight eighteen."

Morgan looked at the monitor again. "That's the same as—"

"Ella Eastman." Beatrice held the form up.

Morgan's mouth fell open as she watched the baseball bat swing over and over, pulverizing the door into an unrecognizable chunk of steel. "She canceled coffee with me this morning."

"Makes sense." Beatrice said.

"Oh my god, they lost a kid." The words fell out of her mouth, in shock from the truth of the situation.

She'd thought the firefighter was ghosting her, too much of a coward to tell her she wasn't interested, but watching Ella lose herself in the release of rage was all she needed to understand why she'd had her coffee alone today.

Morgan couldn't take her eyes off the screen. "And those two work together?" The question was almost a whisper as Ella's arms hammered the targets in the room.

"He brought her in with him."

Morgan didn't hear another word as the pieces of metal broke away and flew against the wall of rage room number one. Ella didn't stop, not for a minute, not even to take a break from smashing every obstacle they'd arranged inside.

"She's going to pass out," Morgan said, mostly to herself. "How much time is left on her room?"

"More than twenty-five minutes."

Morgan walked toward the room Ella was in. "Cut it early. I want to go check on her."

Beatrice flipped the switch, dimming the light in the room, and Morgan saw on her tablet that it took a few moments for Ella to respond. The bat and Ella slid down the wall. Seconds later, Morgan was opening the door.

"Ella?" She called her name, but the music was too loud for either of them to hear anything else. She cut the sound, and the firefighter's head popped up.

Ella blinked a few times in confusion. "What are you doing here?" she asked through tight gasps for air.

"I own this place," Morgan said as she studied the carnage in the room.

Ella's head fell back to rest against the wall. "Yeah, well, I'm glad your business is here." She picked up the bat, clenching the rubber grip with both hands. "It's been a shitty twenty-four hours."

Morgan reached over to take the bat. "Maybe let's have a minute to rest." She watched the firefighter's chest rise and fall as she recovered.

Ella fought to keep the weapon. "No, you don't understand how *shit* this shit day was."

"Yeah, I do." Ella's eyes opened wide as her hands fell into her lap. Morgan tipped the bat to the floor beside her. "Your coworker told us what happened. I'm really sorry."

"Feller has a big ass mouth. He shouldn't have said anything."

"Is that how it works?" Morgan asked, feeling Ella move to put an inch of space between them. Morgan assumed she was raw still, not quite ready to be touched.

"I don't have a lot of people outside of work," Ella explained. "Sure, I know people who aren't firefighters, but it's not the same. Inside the station house, we're family. And what happens there stays there. Otherwise…well, let's just say whatever you bring home can be too much for the people in your life."

Morgan felt connected to this experience. It happened quite often when you ran a place that allowed people to let out anger by bashing inanimate objects. "So you're a loner who buries their pain after a really bad day?"

"Today, I guess I am, but not always. There's just something about kids."

Morgan could read Ella's body language, and it was still screaming, "I don't want to be touched." She had incredible respect for that and pushed up from the floor to stand.

"Why don't you come out in the waiting area so I can reset the room for you?" Morgan asked. "Get a drink of water, and some snacks from the refreshment cart." She held a hand to help Ella up, and she was a little surprised to feel the warm firefighter accept the assistance.

"Thank you," Ella said, her hand lingering a few seconds longer than what Morgan expected.

Morgan did what she would do after any session. She loaded all the debris into a cart, swept the floor, and reset for another session. It was extremely rare for customers to do a back-to-back experience, but after witnessing session one, it was clear Ella needed session number two.

She laid out another vehicle door, which was a perfect target, and she also set out a pair of metal lamps, thinking that breaking glass might be satisfying.

She opened the door, and Ella was there, her coveralls straightened as she downed a bottle of water.

"You ready for round two?" Morgan slid to the side, waving her forward.

"More than." Ella stepped inside, turned to give an apologetic forced smile, and closed the door. Morgan heard the sounds of heavy metal testing the limits of the sound system.

"She's got a lot going on," Beatrice said.

"They lost a kid, B. I'm gonna give her that much." Morgan walked to the room where Lester had just completed his hour. He was standing near the refreshment stand.

"How's Eastman holding up back there?" he asked.

Morgan's and Beatrice's expressions were grim, and Lester seemed to understand that they didn't want to say anything out loud.

"She definitely needs that second session," Beatrice said. "Your girl has some anger issues?" It was as much a question as an observation, but Lester was quick to correct it.

"She's actually pretty solid, and doing stuff like this helps her let go after really horrible days." He took off his gloves and goggles. "We usually hit a batting cage, or she works out, but today I thought your place might be better."

"You see a lot out there?" Beatrice asked as Morgan angled herself so she could watch Ella on the monitor. The vehicle door was pulverized by the new weapon of choice, an eight pound sledge hammer.

"We see it all, and yesterday Eastman was on the girl's extraction. We thought we could save the kid. The parents, they were easy, almost just walked right out." He paused to stare at Ella's monitor. "They didn't even know when they were in the patrol car that their daughter was gone."

"That's horrible," Beatrice said.

"It is."

Morgan didn't hear the rest of the conversation because she was watching Ella's reaction to smashing the first glass lamp. The firefighter was on her knees, head in her palms, maybe crying. It was difficult to tell. Morgan flipped the light switch, knowing there was more than half a session left, but she was compelled to go in, drawn by an unstoppable force to be near this woman, to somehow offer comfort. She cut the audio feed from the hallway.

"Ella?" She said the name, but all she could hear were staggered sobs caught between gasps for air. "Ella?" she repeated with the same result. Her forward steps were guarded, first one, then another, until her hand came to rest on the firefighter's collapsed body.

"Ella?" Morgan whispered as she knelt.

"She was so little," the explanation came out through sobs. "Stupid parents let her…" She trailed off and was silent.

Morgan lost her balance when Ella's body collapsed with hers and shuddering sorrow shook them together. The only thing Morgan could do was hold tight. She didn't know anyone else who sacrificed their best self for the safety of others. This was her welcome to the world of emergency services, and as curious as she was about the woman in her arms, she wasn't sure she could manage a relationship around any more of this.

CHAPTER 7

"Come on princess, give me one more." Marsh had his fingertips near Ella's elbows, giving the lightest touch to guide as she raised the dumbbells. She was working out the grief, like she did, but there was more on her mind than twelve reps at fifty pounds.

"Ahhh," she groaned as the weights pressed to their highest point before she released from the set. She sat forward, resting the dumbbells on her thighs, and lifted her shirt to wipe the sweat from her face. Her biceps burned, but the sensation was exactly what she needed. "You said one more five more ago."

"Well, I need to make sure you're good." Their eyes met in the mirror's reflection.

She shook her head. "Lester call you?" she asked, leaning forward to wipe the bench so Marsh could take his turn.

He shook his head as he fluttered his short shorts before sitting on the bench. "Crumbly came to see me."

"Oh." Wanting to avoid whatever conversation came next, she returned the fifty-pound weights and picked up the seventies.

"She's a sweetie." he said, dimples piercing his cheeks as Ella set the weights in his hands.

"Yeah, she is." A smile fractured the frown lines on her forehead.

He stared at her in the mirror. "G—irl, I could tell you some secrets." He was doing what he did, breaking down her walls with humor, the best weapon he had.

"Can they be better than crumbly?" Ella joked.

He leaned close to his reflection. "You want to know what she does behind the bar at the break of dawn?" The level of mischief in his wink and giggle made his bicep ripple when he picked up the weights.

"Please don't. Oh, gosh, please don't plant any of your naughty thoughts in my mind." She pulled his shoulder back against the bench.

"Cinder-ella, Cinder-ella," he started to sing. "Makes the girls swoon and not the fellas." He raised the weights as she counted.

"One." She smiled, and he raised the weights again. "One." His eyes widened, and he lifted again. "One," she repeated the number five more times, and Marsh was not smiling anymore.

After the eighth count of one, the weights came down to rest on his thighs. "Is that how we're gonna be in the gym today, Cinder-Ella?"

"For a fella like you, it sure the hell is." She pointed at the dumbbells. "Lift 'em Marshy-plumb and show the boys how low that fruit hangs."

He laughed at her, and for the next two hours, Ella disappeared in the solace of routine and the support of friendship.

~~~~~~~~~~

"Rage session? Damn cry session is what it was," Ella grumbled.

She tugged her shirt over her head and the fire department emblem popped out in three dimensions over her breasts. Her wet hair dripped on the dark blue, leaving a discolored mark that looked a little bit like cooking grease spatter. She was frustrated and embarrassed, and that combination continued to a sour the morning. Ella didn't like vulnerability, but she hated public displays of grief even more.

"Give yourself a break, Eastman. It was good for you to let it out." Lester sat on the stainless steel bench beside her, tugging his laces back and forth and hooking the eyelets before tying them. He was the sounding board she needed, but that's what came with twice the experience and double the time in therapy.

"The workout I just finished was good for me, too." She dropped her boots on the floor and held her socks, using them as a pointer to emphasize her words.

"I thought it felt good to smash some shit." His snicker was an irritating punctuation mark on the comment.

Her cheek raised with an encouraging half smile. "It felt fucking incredible."

"So, what's the problem?" He stood and turned to lean against the wall of lockers.

"The shop owner." It was impossible to miss how aggressively Ella slipped into her socks, stretching the elastic to an extreme.

"A pocket-sized human but hot." His smile was teasing, baiting his friend to defend anything different.

Ella, in her frustration, took the bait. "Duh, she's smokin'. And the height difference?" She raised a hand to her shoulder. "It's such a thing for me. But she got a firsthand view of me falling apart. Not hot at all."
~~~~~~~~~~

"She got a good look at the reality of the job you do. She'll either want to know more or she'll let you go." He pushed off the wall and walked away, leaving her to sit in the harsh reality that most women she had an interest in just wanted to let her go.

~~~~~~~~~~

The phone vibrated in her pocket, but Ella's head focused on the job. This was the last cabinet to inventory before she finished a once over of the emergency vehicle. The message could wait. Ten minutes later, she closed the door, tucked the clipboard under her arm, and fished in her pocket for the phone.

Morgan: *I hope today is better for you. She added a little prayer hand emoji.*

Ella's lack of response didn't hinder Morgan's apparent quest to find out how the firefighter was doing. The time stamp displayed a message delivered a few minutes later.

Morgan: *It's okay if you're busy. I just wanted you to know I care and that I'm glad I was there with you and I hope it helped.*

Ella could picture the artist's ink-stained hands moving over the screen to type, and she could also feel the comfort of the hug and the tenderness of the consoling whispered "shh" as small arms held her through the tears.

Morgan: *I'll be at the shop tonight. Someone booked a late session. Come see me when you're off.*

Ella was running through the events of the last hours of her three days on at the station house. The calls were not as overwhelming as the vehicle crash that took the child's life, and
~~~~~~~~~~

the duties of maintenance and station upkeep created the perfect distractions to fight off the imagined bloodstains on her hands from her waking dreams. They never disappeared, but the rage room helped to keep the pile of grief from rising into a mountain.

She had less than an hour until her three days off, and she wasn't sure if seeing Morgan was what she wanted. The artist cared about her for now, and Ella was intrigued, but she also knew that her secret about the convention was just another obstacle between them. She needed to confess and hoped it wasn't the massive lie that she felt it to be. Her thumbs moved across the keyboard of her phone.

Ella: *I'll see you a little after seven*

She dropped the phone in her pocket and ignored it for the rest of the shift. She had to come clean about her cosplay encounter and take her chances that Morgan was the forgiving type.

~~~~~~~~~~

At seven twenty, Ella reached for the knob to open the front door of R.A.T.S. Rage room. She was confused when the door rattled against the frame. It was locked. The window security shades were down, and the small squares of glass on the door were just above her six foot height. From her tip-toes, Ella could peek in at the spotlight lamp on the front desk reception area. Not one person was in sight.

She reached into her pocket for her phone.

Ella: *Out front. Door is locked. Where are you?*

She waited a minute before knocking again. "Morgan!" She called through the solid wood door, assessing how long it
~~~~~~~~~~

might take to kick it in if there was an emergency. She stretched to her toes again for a peek and saw shadows pass in the hallway.

Ella: *Will you please answer the door?*

Seconds later, the service door opened, and Morgan leaned around. Her hair sat atop her head, clumped in a messy bun, faded green spiking out. "I'm so sorry." Her hands flailed franticly. "This door auto locks after seven, and I wasn't thinking." Her finger tapped the side of her head. "I was just in the back resetting a room and lost track of everything." The explanation poured from Morgan in a single breath, and Ella found this character trait quite amusing.

"It's fine. I just didn't expect…" Ella paused because she wasn't sure what she was expecting, not from this bubbly, fascinating person who stood breathless, covered in something flaky and stained brown.

Morgan held out her hand. Ella hesitated for a moment before surrendering to the smaller woman's offer. "Are you feeling strong?" Morgan asked.

The unexpectedly hard tug was all Ella felt as Morgan took off down the hallway to room number four. She propped the rage room door open and wedged a fifty gallon trash can on four caster wheels filled with shards of glass behind it.

"I'm feeling fine, I guess." Hands in her pockets, Ella stood in the doorway.

An oversized dustpan popped up near her belly. "Scoop." Morgan didn't say another word as she picked up the broom to sweep. Ella pushed the can around, collecting all the piles left behind.

"Where is your late customer?" Ella asked, aware for the first time that the two of them were alone in the shop.

"They were a no-show." She shrugged. "It happens, and that's why reservations require a non-refundable deposit." She ticked an imaginary check mark in the air. "It covers my hour here and my art studio is in the building so I can create while I wait. It doesn't matter to me. I can work anywhere." She clipped the broom and dustpan to the trash can and wheeled it into the hall.

Ella thought about the artwork at the convention and imagined Morgan had so much artwork to share. "I'd love to see your studio."

"Yeah?" Morgan opened a new door leading to the storage room, and Ella stopped to take in the contents. "Then I'll take you there next." She reached around Ella and pulled the trash can inside.

"Great, I'd like—" The sight of the storage room was overwhelming. "That's a lot of stuff." She walked to the first rack in the room. There were dozens of shelves, filled to the eight-foot ceiling with labeled bins and crates. "Dishes." She opened up a box and looked inside.

"It's a quick party setup. I like to use dishes when I have a group. Just give them a bucket of baseballs, and depending on accuracy, they have a great time. Sometimes the entire hour leaves behind a floor covered in broken plates."

"Where does all of this come from?" She lifted another lid to find dozens of glass flower vases.

Morgan chuckled. "Dumpsters mostly. There are a few stores in the area that save stuff for me, and I give them a discount if they come in for a rage session."

"Smart." Ella watched as Morgan piled things into a wheeled flatbed cart. "And the car parts? Like the door I smashed last night?"

"Junkyard." She hitched her thumb toward the shopping cart filled with small appliances and a couple of folding chairs. "I network with a couple of people."

"From the looks of this storage room, I would say you network with a *lot* of people." Ella flicked her finger against the glass screen of the thirteen-inch tube TV. "So, what did you need the muscle for?" She raised her arm, playfully flexing her bicep enough to draw the sleeve tight.

Morgan glanced at Ella's arm and, with a flush to her cheeks, was quick to look away. "I wanted to set this up in a room." She patted the top of a flat screen TV. "It's not heavy so much as it's bulky, and a second pair of hands will make moving it faster."

Ella didn't waste the opportunity to slide her arms around the plastic frame and heave it to her hip. "Lead the way."

"Oh." Morgan's breath hitched, mingling with the sound of surprise. "Um, room eight. Through there." She held the storage room door open.

As they walked down the hall, Ella wondered how this warehouse space had become the perfect assemblage of rage rooms. "How'd you put this place together?" She noticed the fire extinguisher on the wall and lingered on the currently dated inspection tag.

"The rooms?"

Ella shook her head as she lifted the TV onto the pedestal of cinder blocks. "The building. This maze of cubical cubbies laid out in almost the perfect design to accommodate flying debris from glass and steel?" She dusted the front of her jeans.

"The building was constructed during the nuclear scare days, and they fortified all of these rooms to withstand bombs or something like that." Her hand gave a casual, circular wave to encompass all the space. "Anyway, it was a mess the first time I came in."

"So you rebuilt all of this?" Ella leaned against the wall, waiting as Morgan laid out an aluminum bat and a sledgehammer.

"B and I did. She's the architect, and a sort of business partner, but she still has a regular day job." Morgan pointed down the hall at the office door. "If you need a brilliant accountant, she's got you covered."

"That's amazing. Did you meet in college?"

Morgan held a hand, guiding the two of them out of the room and down the hall to the gift shop and front office space. "We actually met in a chat room."

"Over the internet?"

Ella followed her through a door into an industrial elevator. The outer gate pulled up from the floor and down from the ceiling like a giant mouth closing around to devour them. Her hands pressed flat to the wall as Morgan pushed the *up* button on the dented steel two button panel box. In her head, Ella crossed her fingers that they'd make it to the second floor.

"No stairs?"

"There are," Morgan confirmed, "but at the end of the day, I'm sometimes too tired to climb them."

The ride was slow, and Ella could see the cracked stucco of the elevator shaft through the slatted cage lifting them.

"Oh, and yes," Morgan said. "Beatrice and I met over the internet chatting about the *Brodies* TV show."

"That's right, I saw your character cards at the con," Ella said casually, and then the reality of that weekend returned. Morgan wouldn't remember their interaction because she was in costume, completely disguised and unknown to the world as Ella.

"You did?" Morgan looked confused.

The elevator stopped, and she stepped out into a small, open lobby space. Ella hesitated as she felt the hitch and lurch of the lifting stop.

"I did."

Morgan looked confused. "I don't remember seeing you before leaving the theater. When were you at my table?" She was digging in her pocket for keys.

"That first day."

As she followed Morgan into the landing space, she noticed two chairs sat on each side of the elevator. Ella could see a second door at the end of the hall, but Morgan stopped at door number one.

The entrance opened into a large kitchen with a dining table big enough for four people to eat together. The exterior wall wasn't a wall so much as it was floor to ceiling glass windows surrounded by steel paint-pocked framing. It was certainly old and industrial, but it fit the artist vibe Morgan lived by, and to Ella it felt like a home.

"This place is so great." Her excited voice echoed off the high ceilings. Someone had taken the time to paint everything above them white and the room reflected off it, making it feel endless.

"It's a work in progress." Morgan led her to the patchwork of fabric hanging behind the worn sofa. "And back here, this is the studio." She held the curtain aside, revealing an artist's dream space. The first thing Ella saw was the packed crates with a few prints she recognized from the show. The next thing she noticed was the horizontal doors repurposed into tables, covered with colorful drawings and trays filled with pencils and sketching charcoal.

Ella didn't know what to say.

"It's not fancy." Morgan said, sounding embarrassed.

"Fancy." Ella stepped for a closer look at the obvious work in progress of the Arsonist. "This is outstanding. I've never seen anything like it." She wasn't talking about the art so much as the space for creating it. "If this was my studio, I'd never leave." She saw the sewing machines in the corner. "You sew, too?"

She smiled. "I make almost everything I need for the rage rooms, so yes, I sew, too."

"Talented and beautiful," Ella whispered, but she'd meant to keep the observation in her head. She blushed when she realized Morgan had heard her thinking out loud.

"Thank you."

"You're welcome. And wow, Morgan. This place is insane."

"I like it, too. And the commute is nothing." They walked back to the area with the couch and coffee table.

"I'd love to just walk down a flight of stairs to my job." Ella looked at the box they'd ridden up in. "Or an elevator." She had a moment of wonder, thinking about what Marsh had said about climbing stairs at the Sage Lounge and Morgan's comment in the elevator about navigating the stairs. "What you said earlier, about being tired at the end of the day. What's that about?" She turned to look at the flashing lights reflected off the window glass.

Morgan's hands rubbed across her thighs. She looked uncertain, like she was worried about how Ella would react to what she had to say. "When I was a kid, I had an accident."

Ella's head turned toward Morgan. For the firefighter, accidents were a daily thing. Some were simple things like a trip and fall, but many were like the scene that brought her to the rage room. She saw the pain of grief shadow Morgan's expression as a glossy sheen clouded her eyes.

"Car?" Ella asked.

Morgan shook her head. "Fire."

Ella slid closer on the couch until her hand came to rest on Morgan's. Firefighting was in her blood. She lived and breathed her job, but it was extremely rare to know the outcome of most calls. You show up, do your job, load the victims, and return to the station. That was usually the end.

Morgan was on the other side, the victim's side.

"It's okay if you don't want to tell me." She squeezed Morgan's hand but didn't let it go.

"I was eleven," she said. "Gosh, almost twenty years ago now." She used her other hand to swipe away a tear. "I was visiting my grandma for the summer." It was clear she struggled with the memory, so long removed but still alive in her mind.

"If it's too hard, you don't have to." *Why did I have to go and pry?* Ella asked herself as she watched the artist's struggle.

"It's fine, Ella. It was a long time ago, but sometimes when I talk about that day, it feels like yesterday."

"It's never really gone, is it?"

Morgan forced a pained smile, confirming the truth in her words. "Grammy." She giggled when she said the name. "I called her grammy. It was just for me, though, and she loved the nickname." It was obvious by the way Morgan's eyes gleamed that the bond was a special one. "Grammy was making popcorn. Gosh, something so innocent when you think about it." She paused again as the memory replayed for her. "Grammy raised the lid. She made it the old-fashioned way, as she called it. A giant pool of grease in a pot and lots of kernels. Somehow the pot tipped sideways, and before we could do anything, the grease was over the stovetop, spilling all over, catching her nightgown and my pajamas on fire."

Ella's arm came around to hold Morgan's trembling body. "You don't have to say anything else. I know what a grease fire can do."

But Morgan was obviously lost in the feelings, in the screams and cries of pain, retelling the details of that horrible night. "I don't know how she did it, but grammy smothered the flames on my legs while she was covered in second-and third-degree burns." Morgan tensed as Ella rubbed her shoulder. "Her neighbor was coming home from work and saw the fire through the window, or so I was told. I was in a coma for two days, and the next thing I remembered was a few weeks later when she died from the burns."

"Oh, Morgan. I'm so sorry." Ella felt terrible for bringing up the memories.

"Yeah. I don't talk about it very much, but I think I owe you after the other day."

"We're quite a pair." Ella turned up her palm, offering her hand.

Morgan stared at the calloused skin, looking grateful for it. "I guess we are."

"I told her about the fire," Morgan said as she pulled the door of the gift shop open, catching Beatrice in the doorway. They were counting inventory to change out seasonal clothes and restock the shelves with the artwork Morgan removed for the convention.

Beatrice stopped. "Wait, you did what?"

"Ella came by last night, and she's so damn observant and such a good listener that she asked about my need for the elevator, and I felt so comfortable that I told her about Grammy and the fire." She gulped a breath of air.

"And your legs?" B asked.

"She knows I was burned. I'm sure she has experience with the kind of scars second- and third-degree burns leave behind."

Beatrice picked up the fluffy dusting pom-pom and swiped across the bookshelf near the door. "So you didn't show her?"

"Uh, it was hardly a second date. I kept my pants on."

Beatrice laughed before asking, "Did she?"

The shoulder smack that followed was more like a love tap, but Morgan knew Beatrice would understand that the subject needed to change.

"Is she at least a good kisser?"

Morgan's back was turned when she answered. "I don't know." She opened the safe in the wall and removed the cash bag from the day before.

"You didn't kiss the hot firefighter?" She waved her hand to smack her friend back. "Why didn't you kiss the hot firefighter?"

"It's not because I didn't want to, and stop calling her that." The tug on the cash bag zipper mirrored the frustration in her tone. "I think I freaked her out."

Beatrice took the paper bills from the bag and began to sort and count the piles. "She's seen fires before, duh. What would freak her out?"

"I kinda fell apart." Morgan stacked the coins into individual denominations that were easy to count.

"Oh, how bad?" She stopped adjusting the faces on the bills to look at her friend.

"Like shoulder booger and slobber bad."

"You didn't."

Morgan made a note of the coin count value and scooped each pile into the cupped portions of the cash register drawers. "All over her shirt. It was gross and so embarrassing." She sidestepped so Beatrice could tuck the smaller bills into the drawer. "She's never going to call again."

"I'm sorry, Morg." B's arm draped over her shoulder. "You can still be my third wheel. Rowan doesn't mind."

"That's because Rowan is too nice for their own good." She pushed hard to close the drawer.

"They are, aren't they?"

Morgan checked the inventory on the shelves. "You're lucky you're not in the dating world. It's so scary out there." She opened a drawer, removed two large t-shirts and put them on hangers.

"Rowan is good for me, that's for sure." She took the shirts and hung them behind the mediums, filling the gap on the rack. "But I think the firefighter is gonna call. The two of you made a connection."

"A connection?" Morgan laughed. "What are you now, the love doctor?"

At that moment, the phone beside the cash register buzzed. Beatrice scooted around the counter and picked it up. "Or maybe the firefighter will text."

Morgan snatched the phone before B could read it.

Ella: *I can't stop worrying about you. How are you this morning?*

Morgan stared at the screen. It was clear she didn't know a thing about dating and even less about what this woman thought about her. Maybe she could save herself some embarrassment if she ignored the texts. She decided an honest response might scare her off. She began to type.

Morgan: *Don't worry, I've been doing this all of my life.*
Morgan studied the screen, hesitant to hit the send button until Ella sent another text.

Ella: *I know you've been living with the memory all of your life. I wanted you to know I'm thinking about you.*

Morgan hit the delete button over and over until her previous message was gone.
Ella: *Don't feel pressured, but I'm off today if you want to have lunch or go do something?*

The text messages were a thousand times better than a call. She had written confirmation that her past hadn't frightened the firefighter away.

Morgan: *Come by at noon. We can eat upstairs. I can take a break for a few hours.*
Ella: *See you then*

Morgan watched the clock for the first hour the store was open. She took three phone calls and scheduled more than a dozen rage room visits from their website. Time was at a standstill, and she wondered what force of nature slowed the passage of time to torture her today.

"You know a watched pot never boils, don't you?" Beatrice said, clutching a pile of papers to her chest.

"Ahh! Why did you have to read over my shoulder? I'm nervous enough as it is."

"She's interested," B assured her. "You should be happy."

"I want to be happy, but she's interested, and that's a little bit scary."

Beatrice walked out of the shop. As she passed the clock, she pointed to it. "Thirty-five minutes and counting."

CHAPTER 8

"I was thinking about spending the time outdoors," Ella said as she locked the car and walked down the sidewalk. To passers-by it might appear she was talking to herself, but the dangling cord connecting her ear bud to the phone was a sanity identifier, at least at a second glance.

"With mobility restrictions?" Lester asked. She'd told him about Morgan's accident and about the physical changes to her legs.

"There's a cool path up to Spring Falls. Maybe we can try it."

She'd searched the internet for outdoor walking paths that also maintained accessible access for wheelchair users and people with other physical limits. She wanted to be outside, open her lungs to fresh air and maybe escape the space where she felt confined.

"You should ask her first." His coaching was adorable and attentive for a guy who talked like a player but was married to the same person for over fifteen years.

"I was planning to." She turned the corner and smiled when she saw the *Open* sign blinking in the window of the rage room gift shop. "I'm here. I gotta go, man."

She didn't wait for him to say goodbye; she was too busy crossing the street. If she was being honest with herself, she really liked this woman, and every bit of her wanted to get to know more about her. The cord of her headphones dangled as she twirled them around her phone and stuffed the wad into her back pocket.

The brass bells over the door tingled when Ella opened it to enter. Morgan was there, sitting behind the register, and the smile that greeted Ella was confirmation that the attraction was mutual.

"Hi," Ella said and gave herself a dozen internal slaps for lameness.

"Hi back." Morgan put her pencil down and walked around the counter. Their face-to-face greeting was awkward until she asked, "Is a hug okay?"

Ella's smile was the perfect answer as she opened her arms. With their height difference, Morgan didn't quite fit against her. Their bodies connected in awkward places, but she held on until Morgan let go. Hugs were an important way for Ella to connect with people. When they meant something, she held on as long as possible.

"You feeling—"

Morgan cut off the question. "I'm glad you texted. I thought maybe my slobber all over you might have scared you away."

Ella's brief laugh was followed by, "I experience a lot of body fluids, Morgan. I didn't mind yours at all."

"To an outsider, that statement sounds kinda gross, and maybe a little kinky." She pinched her finger together, leaving a tiny gap as a physical example.

Ella shrugged. "Maybe, but it's also true." She wandered around the gift shop, touching the logo printed shirts and hats. She picked up a mini baseball bat stamped with the phrase, "I hit it hard at R.A.T.S.: the rooms to rage in."

"This is so great," Ella said. "I might need one of these for my car."

"Really?"

"For the passengers who can't keep their hands off the radio." She slapped it against her palm before putting it back on the shelf. Ella continued her survey of the shop. "There's some fun stuff in here." She held up a crocheted bullet-proof vest. Her eyebrow raised with a question mark grin.

"Everyone needs soft body armor, right?"

Ella shook her head and placed it back on the shelf. "No one I know." She made her way back to Morgan.

"He's a local artist. A lot of the stuff in the shop is made by people working a side hustle. I'm lucky enough to have a space for them." Morgan leaned against the tall side of the check-out counter where she'd been working on a new sketch.

"So I was thinking maybe we could have lunch *outside*." It was less of a question, but Ella hung on the last word.

"Like at my rooftop table?" Morgan asked.

"Well, maybe if I'd known about that, I would have suggested it, but I was thinking a little walk to a place you might like."

Morgan shifted her weight from one foot to the other, looking anxiously at the clock. Ella wasn't sure exactly what she was thinking, but she could guess.

"How far is this walk?" Morgan asked.

"A mile in and a mile out, and maybe a half mile wandering." Ella hesitated before asking, "Is that too much?"

"I have a full schedule in the rooms. A mile in is only halfway. What's the terrain like?"

Ella stood next to Morgan, shoulder to shoulder. Well, *almost* shoulder to shoulder. "It's a path, not a trail," she explained as she opened the pictures on her phone. "I choose paths like this because I can do them after a tough shift. Kind of a well-marked escape that I can just do and not have to think about."

Morgan looked at the screen captures Ella had taken from the website. "It's paved?"

"Almost all the way to the falls."

Morgan walked behind the counter and picked up the shop phone. She pressed a button and seconds later, she said, "Can you cover the shop?" She was silent for a beat, waiting for an answer.

"Hot firefighter?" the voice on the other end asked. It sounded like Beatrice.

Morgan looked at Ella, who stood opposite to her with adoring and hopeful eyes. "Yep." Her voice sounded a little squeaky.

"Go have a good time." Ella could hear laughter coming from her friend. "Maybe try not to keep your pants on."

"Mm hmm."

"She's standing right there, isn't she?" Beatrice said.

"Yep," she squeaked again.

"Maybe just kiss her. Pants are optional."

"Goodbye." Morgan dropped the phone on the base. "Let's take that walk." Morgan grabbed the canvas bag hanging on the wall behind the desk. She closed her sketch pad and placed her art supplies with it in a drawer. "You ready for lunch?"

"I've been ready for a while," Ella said with a smile.

She held out a hand, and Morgan didn't hesitate to take hold as they left the shop. They walked the block to Ella's car, and Morgan did her best wolf whistle when they stopped to open the door.

"This is yours?" Morgan's fingertips traveled the contoured side of the powder-blue car.

"Sure is. Charlene and I have a long history."

Morgan's smile was curious. "You named your car."

Ella shook her head as she unlocked the door and opened it for Morgan. "Charlene is more than a car. She's my gorgeous, gorgeous lady. We hardly ever fight, and she's stayed with me through all the hard times. Haven't you, baby?" She rubbed the soft top of the roof.

Morgan slid into the seat, and as Ella walked around, they each watched the other. "Passionate about the ladies?" she asked when the driver's door opened.

"I am, but I'm particularly fond of this one." Ella's hand caressed the dashboard. "My grandmother's partner restored her, and they left her to me."

"Your grandmother was queer?" Morgan asked.

"As queer as me. Probably more because she was already with Lou when they were my age. 'Best friends for life.'" Ella made quotation marks in the air before laughing at how ridiculous it was to say now.

"So, how did your parents come into the picture if they were a couple?"

"Going for the life history before I even start the car," Ella teased, but answered before Morgan could respond. "They were my foster parents. A retired school teacher and a twenty-year military vet. They looked great on paper, and that's all that mattered back then."

"So, you were in foster care?" Morgan asked.

Ella started the car and shifted into gear. "I wasn't in foster care, not really. My grandmother was actually my godmother and best friends with my parents. When they passed, she got me in the will."

"Quite the family history."

Ella shrugged. "I guess, but I had a good childhood. I was six when my parents died, so I only really remember Grandmother and Lou."

"And Charlene here was Lou's baby?"

Ella smiled as she laughed. "You're gettin' it now."

"It's very nice to meet you, Charlene."

Morgan rubbed the powder blue dash, and Ella kicked back in her seat to enjoy the short drive to the park.

Morgan was hyperaware of many things when it came to her body. She knew she wasn't an athlete, but independence was connected to mobility, and she wanted every level of movement she could get. She walked as much as possible to keep the scars from ruling her life. The burns took too much already.

"We're almost there," Ella said as she circled through the gate, paused so the ranger could see her annual pass in the window, and proceeded to the parking lot for the falls.

"So you're a big hiker?" Morgan asked, and for the first time, she was aware of the difference in their physical abilities.

"Massive, I'd say." Ella shifted into park, set the emergency brake, and threw her arm over the bench seat to turn and face Morgan. "You don't have to worry. You set the pace, okay? I can follow, too."

Morgan released the breath she wasn't aware she was holding. The bag at her feet was a reminder that this could go either way. "I set the pace?"

"You're in charge, Morgan Hail."

With that simple sentence, Morgan flipped the door release and slid out of the car. She could do this. Today was a good day. By the time she had the sling bag over her shoulder, Ella was there with a backpack and a stainless steel bottle of water on her hip.

"After you." Ella swung her arm toward the asphalt path.

"Maybe we can just walk side by side." Morgan hooked Ella's fingers as she passed, dragging the six-foot firefighter up next to her. "You don't strike me as the following kind."

"That easy to see, huh?"

Morgan chuckled. "Ella Eastman, nothing about you seems easy."

Ella threw her hands over her heart, stumbling and staggering sideways. "Ah, you wound me."

"You look like you can take a hit." Morgan tapped Ella's belly, feeling the hard body underneath. She stopped along the grass of the path and opened her bag, removed the collapsible walking sticks, twisted them to her height, and tossed her bag back over her shoulder. "I hope you can keep up, oh wounded one." She winked and began the mile walk to their waterfall destination.

"I'm on your right," Ella joked, and they enjoyed the steady climb up the ridged path.

Morgan was proud of herself for the pace she was keeping. It'd been a while since she'd done something like this, but it felt good. Invigorating. And she was enjoying the view as they hiked–both the scenery *and* the woman next to her.

"Are you hungry?" Ella asked at one point.

"Not yet, but I'm working up an appetite." Morgan gave a playful wink and trekked her poles against the surface of the path.

"I thought maybe we could just stroll a bit."

Morgan stopped. "Stroll?"

"Yeah, stroll. Like talk about life and Mother Nature. Maybe you could tell me about your art. Stuff like that."

"We kinda talked about a lot of that already," Morgan reminded her. "Maybe you could tell me about why you became a firefighter?"

"You ask like there's a story there. I'm not...it's not a family thing. Not in my bloodline or anything like that."

Morgan kept walking. "So what is it?"

"Don't laugh," she said hesitantly.

"I wouldn't."

"It kinda felt like a calling."

Morgan stopped, turning to look at Ella. "I don't think there's anything funny about it. Not at all. You run towards danger when everyone else runs away." She dropped her pole, the wrist strap holding tight as it dangled from her raising hand. She touched Ella's cheek. "It isn't funny at all, Ella Eastman."

They stood there for a long moment, each staring into the other's eyes. Morgan licked her lips, her focus zeroing in on kissing Ella. A hiker passed beside them, bumping into Ella, who hit Morgan, knocking her off balance and forcing her to the ground. Morgan's trekking poles flipped sideways as Ella dropped to her knees.

"Are you hurt?" Ella asked in concern. Then she looked over her shoulder to yell at the hiker, "Hey, asshole, be more careful next time. What the hell, man!" She turned back to see Morgan's sour expression. "What?"

"That wasn't necessary."

"What part, calling him out or calling him an asshole?"

"Both maybe." She pushed off the ground, careful of her knee. The scar tissue was heavy on the left side, and unfortunately, that's where she'd landed. It was going to leave a mark.

"Are you hurt?"

"Only my pride." She rubbed her knee and felt the sting from the hard landing.

"Come over here and sit down." Ella's hands came up to take Morgan's, and she led her toward a large boulder on the path.

Morgan tried not to limp.

"You are hurt," Ella said, and without hesitation, she tugged the poles from Morgan's wrists, scooped her up, and carried her the last ten feet to sit her on the rock.

"You don't need to carry me," Morgan insisted. But she liked being in Ella's arms, liked feeling her nearness. It was comforting.

When Ella set Morgan down, Morgan saw blood seeping through the light fabric of her cotton pants.

"You're bleeding," Ella said, clearly worried.

Morgan covered the patch of red that was growing. "It'll be fine. It's the scars. They're just weird on that side. Any minor bump can be like that." She tried very hard to downplay the injury, knowing that her claim wasn't true. She'd need to ice it soon, and as she stared at the path ahead, she knew it would be impossible to do that if they continued.

"That was *not* a minor bump." Ella's tone had changed, and Morgan realized this must be her first responder voice kicking in "We need to look at it."

"No, we don't." She pushed Ella's hands away. "I know my body. It'll be fine when I ice it later."

"Blood." Ella pointed out the obvious growing red stain.

"It's just a scrape." She slid off the rock and back onto her feet. "It'll be okay, but maybe we should skip the rest of the walk and head back down."

"You're sure? I still think we should treat your injury before we go anywhere."

"I'm sure. Just grab the poles and we can get on it."

Ella looked doubtful, then a small smile crossed her lips. She picked up the poles and collapsed them, stuffing them both in the bag on her back. Then she flipped the bag to fit over her chest and backed her body right up to the rock. "Climb on." Ella looked over her shoulder at Morgan.

"Um, no. No way are you carrying me out."

"Either you ride my front or you ride my back, but either way, I'm carrying you off of this trail."

Morgan looked down at her knee. "Ella, please."

"Look." She squatted down and touched Morgan's chin so she could look in her eyes. "I know you could march right out of here. I know it, but you don't have to."

Morgan looked away, embarrassed.

"I promise I'll keep you safe," Ella said.

Morgan stared at the bloodstain on her leg. She knew it was the right thing to do, but asking for help was never easy. She'd gotten to almost thirty by forging ahead. Giving in felt like giving up.

"We can tackle this walk another day, I promise." Ella crossed her fingers over her heart.

Morgan held up her pinkie. "Promise?"

Ella hooked their pinkie fingers together. "Promise."

Maybe it could *be that simple*, Morgan thought as she stared at the taller woman. "I'll get on, but only if you let me wear the backpack."

"Are you sure?"

"Only way I'll do it." Her arms crossed in front of her, she held the ultimate I'm-not-budging position.

Ella took the bag off her chest and held tight as she passed it to Morgan, who realized it was heavier than it looked. Small but mighty, Morgan grabbed hold and tossed it on. Ella looked impressed and held her arms open to Morgan.

"Front or back?" She turned to point with her thumb at her shoulder.

"I'll take the back. That way it'll look like we're on a date."

Ella's face fell, just for a moment. "Oh, I thought we were." Then she helped Morgan onto her back.

~~~~~~~~~~~

The elevator to the second floor never looked so good as the jaws of the door closed down, lifting the two of them to the apartment space above. Morgan tried to ignore that Ella couldn't take her eyes off of the stain of blood on Morgan's knee. Their trip had started so well, and Morgan was embarrassed that one little stumble screwed it up.

She couldn't stand the silence, and Ella seemed uncomfortable, too. The elevator lurched to a stop, and Morgan did her best to hide a limp as she walked toward the refrigerator to get ice from the freezer. She could put that on without revealing the scars on her legs.

"Will you let me look at the cut now?" Ella asked with the most compassionate whisper. "I don't care about your scars."
~~~~~~~~~~~

Morgan's eyes opened wide. "Maybe *you* don't, but I do." She leaned against the kitchen countertop.

Before Morgan could say another word, Ella was up against her, hands on each hip. They were a breath apart. Morgan's heart hammered in her chest, hard and fast, and all she wanted to do was answer the question of how soft Ella's lips could be. Morgan felt Ella dip down, but the touch she expected changed into an effortless lift from the floor to the countertop. The move was one of the hottest experiences in her recent memories, and the small gasp that escaped her mouth was evidence that Ella had caught her off guard.

"I didn't hurt you, did I?" Ella asked.

Morgan could only shake her head, afraid a verbal answer would come out like a squeaking mouse.

"Can I roll up your pant leg?"

Morgan nodded. She was exhausted and invigorated at the same time, and the crashing together of those two emotions left her feeling vulnerable.

With gentle hands, Ella turned a cuff at the ankle and folded the material. Her expression didn't change as she revealed the first glimpse of scarring. Fold after fold, the fabric turned until she felt it pull against the dried blood.

Morgan waited for a reaction: repulsion, disgust, or even a flinch, but Ella only said. "I'm sorry, but this might hurt a little bit."

Morgan finally found her voice. "It won't hurt. The nerves were damaged. It's the swelling that bothers the non-damaged part." Her hip rotated so Ella could push up the clump of fabric to reveal the wound.

"First aid kit?"

"Cabinet over the sink." She pointed, and Ella had no problem opening the grey-washed double doors that Morgan needed a step stool to reach.

"Wash cloth?"

With that question, Morgan surrendered to the scene. There was no bias in the way Ella was caring for her, just the action of a trained caregiver, and as she leaned back to shift her bodyweight on the counter, she was willing to receive the attention offered in kindness.

"Bathroom, through my bedroom." She pointed at the closed door, and the firefighter disappeared, returning a few seconds later with two towels.

For the next few minutes, the women said nothing. They were patient and caregiver, and both were content with their positions. Ella's calloused hands were gentle but deft, laying out just enough wound care to dress the two inch long gouge in her knee. Morgan was fascinated, and if it was possible to find comfort in the moment, she felt safe.

"How's it feel?"

Morgan kicked her foot side to side, an awkward twist that flexed her knee. "Feels like I took a fall and whacked the crap out of my knee."

"Sounds about right." Ella's hands reached to turn the long folds of fabric down, but a warm hand stopped her progress. Although long healed, the scars were impossible to miss.

"Thank you." Morgan used her right leg to push the cuff past her shin and cover the last bit of bare skin.

From the height of the counter, they were face to face, and the look in Ella's eyes was the most vulnerable expression of concern. "For what?"

"For seeing them." She pointed at her leg with a head tilt. "And for not seeing them."

Ella leaned against the counter, her elbow landing a few inches from Morgan's thigh. "I see you, Morgan Hail. We all have scars. Some are just easier to see than others."

It would have been the perfect moment to close her eyes and kiss the woman, but she didn't, and part of her wondered if it would ever happen.

"Can I help you down?"

Morgan nodded, and firm hands wrapped around her waist. Their bodies slid together, and Ella held tight, making sure Morgan was solidly on her feet.

"We never got to have that picnic."

Ella walked toward the elevator. "Maybe you can write me a rooftop raincheck?" She opened the elevator jaws, stepped inside, and closed them.

"How about we try that trail again?" Morgan stood in front of the slatted door. Most of her weight shifted to the right leg. She wasn't going hiking for a couple of days.

Ella winked. "After next shift." Her finger pressed the down button.

"I'll see you in a few days." The elevator lurched and began a slow descent.

"See you soon." She pointed at Morgan's knee. "You better get some ice on that." The hum of the elevator filled the space left behind by an adorable firefighter.

CHAPTER 9

"Would you like to have dinner?" Ella asked, phone gripped tight in her hand.

It had been a week since their waterfall mishap, but they'd talked and texted whenever they could. Morgan's knee was healing, and their in-person dates were simple talks in Morgan's apartment or quiet dinners on her rooftop. The furniture wasn't much, just a salvaged picnic table and some chairs, but it was intimate and private, and they had time to be together, alone.

"Late on the roof?" Morgan asked. "My last rage ends at seven."

Ella laid on her back, her body stretched out on the locker room bench. "What are you hungry for?"

"Surprise me." Ella could hear Morgan's smile over the phone.

Ella hung up the phone, cheeks flushed, a smile lighting her face as she sat up and closed the locker with "Eastman" taped on the front. *Work first*, she thought as she put her head into the last three hours of her four day shift. She'd call the Sage Lounge and order dinner. It had been a very long time since she'd thought about a woman and an even longer time since she'd wanted to spend time with only one.

"Eastman!" Lester called as the alarm blared in the station. The time for day dreaming was over. "Head in it, Cinder!"

"Let's go, Probie!" Her boots pounded against the cold concrete as she kicked out to step into her turnouts and launch into the rig. "Head in it."

It was her last thought as she ran through the procedure for their auto versus pedestrian call.

〜〜〜〜〜〜〜〜

"Fucking stop lights are for stopping." She fell onto the locker room bench as she popped the buttons on her sweat-soaked uniform shirt.

"You did good out there, Eastman," their department captain said as he walked by and patted her shoulder. "Damn good!" The compliment echoed off the glass walls as he entered his office and closed the door.

"Damn, Cinder. You were everywhere with that lady." The station was buzzing with compliments from the rest of her team. She was doing her job, just like every other firefighter on the scene.

"Yeah, well, that drunk asshole was enough for the rest of you to handle." She grabbed Les's cheek and tipped his face to the left. "How's the eye?"

The drunk driver who'd struck the pedestrian put up a fight as the police arrived, preventing most of the team from assessing his passenger. Ella had control of the solitary woman whose head injury looked like a Halloween horror event. She'd immobilized the unconscious victim, single-handedly backboarded her, and when the second ambulance arrived, she helped them load the woman into the vehicle and remove her from the scene.

Ella had walked up to the car just in time to catch Lester before the punch to his face knocked him to the ground. Their probie, Wilson, watched more than he helped, and they'd have to talk about his failure to act.

"I'll be fine. Ice and a nap are all I need." Lester looked up at the clock on the wall. "Don't you have a hot date?"

It was well past seven, closer to eight-thirty. She grabbed her phone from the shelf in her locker and held it for Lester to see. "Five messages."

"Maybe she'll understand." He tossed his shirt into a duffle bag and fiddled with the strap over his shoulder.

Ella shook her head. "They never understand." She unlocked her phone and read the first text message.

Morgan: *I hope everything is okay?*

She'd sent the message at seven fifteen. It made sense to check on the punctual firefighter. Usually she sent a heads up if she was going to be late. Ella walked to her car, reading the next message as she fished in her pocket for car keys.

Morgan: *If you're at a call, please be safe.*

The second message arrived at seven twenty-two. It wasn't a panicked message, but it was clear Morgan cared. Ella would need to talk about radio silence on the job and let her know that she didn't always have access to her phone. She jabbed the key in the lock to open the car, dropped her duffle on the passenger side as she whispered, "Damn, Charlene. I think I kinda blew it." She put the key in the ignition.

Morgan: *just wanted to say I'm hungry, and I made us dinner. Please come when you can.*

Ella felt a pang of guilt as she read the message. Her plans for spicy wings and chili chips from the Sage Lounge were destroyed. This was the job. You go when you're called and you stay til you're finished. No one ever stuck around for her with a life like that.

Morgan: *Dinner is warm, I'm kinda cold on the roof. Please, no matter what, come and see me.*

That message was sent at seven forty-five. Ella frowned at the thought of sweet Morgan, the kind and tough woman waiting on the roof for her to show up. At five after eight she'd sent one last message.

Morgan: *I'll be working in the gift shop. Let me know when you're coming.*

Ella thought for a moment about what she wanted to say. She should have taken the time to shower or change out of her clothes. She should have. It was never wise to leave the way she had. Her thumbs moved over the keyboard on her phone.

Ella: *Just finished a call. I'm filthy and need a shower. Maybe I should just see you tomorrow?*

She hit the send button and expected to wait for a reply. Morgan apparently had other ideas because her response was almost immediate.

Morgan: *Come to the shop. I'm still here and we should talk.*

The tone of the last message had certainly changed. Ella pumped the gas a few times, started the car, and drove the few blocks to Morgan's place. The *Open* sign was turned off, and the only light she could see as she stood on her toes was the one over the counter where Morgan sat sketching. She knew what the artist looked like at work, her focused furrowed brow, the tip of her tongue between her teeth. It was charming. That's not what Ella saw.

Morgan sat at her computer, and the flash of a monitor screen kept her attention.. Ella blinked hard when she saw a photograph and not an artist's sketch. She recognized the picture. It was the group shot at the convention, the one with Dracea Barnes. The one with Ella dressed in her award-winning Arsonist cosplay.

The tone of the last text message made sense to her now. The truth was out, and from the serious expression on Morgan's face, she wasn't happy at all.

Picture after picture, like after like, little love heart emojis compiled by over two hundred thousand followers. *This has to be some kind of cosmic joke*, she thought as her phone buzzed on the counter in front of her, but she sat focused on the social media page of @Cinder_EllaE.

Ella: *I'm outside*

The message alert popped up in the corner of her computer screen and she paused, scrolling to read it. She didn't reply, just stood to cross the gift shop and open the door. Ella wasn't standing in front of it. She opened the door wider, and the tall firefighter was leaning against the wall, her booted foot kicked up on the bricks.

"What are you doing?" Morgan asked.

Ella turned, her arms crossed over her chest. "I was trying to decide if I should just cut my losses and go home."

That response got Morgan's attention. "Cut your losses?"

"I could see you through the window. You were looking at my social media pages, weren't you?"

Morgan let out a quick frustrated laugh. "Cinder Ella, huh?"

"I'll just go." She pushed off the wall.

"So you knew exactly who I was when you asked me that question about the premiere?"

Ella's hands were jammed deep into her pockets as she turned to answer. "I didn't mean to…I wanted to tell you…it all happened so fast and then…" She was obviously struggling to figure out what to say.

"Will you come inside?" Morgan pulled the door wide enough for the firefighter to enter. "I'm willing to listen if you're ready to tell me why."

"Are you sure?"

She stepped back, holding tight to the handle. "Just come in." She waved a frustrated hand toward the empty shop.

Ella stood for a moment; the strong, tough woman was also ashamed and vulnerable. Then she nodded like she was making a decision and followed after Morgan. Morgan didn't say a word as she returned to her workspace. She sat in her chair and wiggled the mouse to wake the sleeping screen. "You want to tell me about this?"

She enlarged the photograph of Ella in a Santa suit from December of last year. The firefighter had on a pointed hat with fluffy white trim. The boots were regulation except for the candy cane striped fur around the tops. That wasn't what caught Morgan's eye. What she'd noticed, and what she was certain anyone would, was the red velvet crop top that left Ella's extremely carved abdominals visible.

"Miss December: Put out that chimney fire, and she'll deliver all of your Christmas dreams," Morgan read the description at the bottom of the social media post.

Ella pointed a finger toward her mouth, making a gagging sound as she did. "Work calendar. The photo's great, but the description is awful."

"And this one?" Morgan switched to a picture of The Arsonist with a little girl dressed in a similar but very homemade costume.

"That was a kid I met at the con," Ella explained with a small smile. "She loved the costume."

"And this?"

Ella's smile faded at the image of her in cosplay sans helmet with the star who played the Arsonist on the show. "That was a meet and greet with Dracea Barnes."

"You're the cosplayer?" Morgan knew her voice sounded angry and a little bit sad.

"I'm sorry," Ella said. And she looked it, too. But Morgan was still upset.

"For what? For making me feel foolish or for lying about it all this time?"

"It wasn't like that." She dropped into the empty chair. "I tried to tell you at the Sage that night. And on the hike. But we were just clicking, and I enjoy being with you, and suddenly days turned into weeks, and I didn't know how to bring it up anymore."

"You should have told me." She scrolled the wheel on her mouse, scanning hundreds of posts, finally clicking to bring up one more picture.

"I know, but you have to believe me when I tell you I didn't mean to hurt you."

"I learned a lot about you on here." She didn't look at Ella as she continued scrolling through. She'd spent most of the waiting hour looking through Ella's social page. "I think this one is my favorite." The mouse pointer stopped, and she clicked to fill the monitor screen.

Ella rested her head in her hand as she turned to look. She'd linked her social media to her cosplay and that fundraising firefighter's calendar, but the photograph on the screen was of Ella's body, silhouetted as she posed atop a cliff, surrounded by mountains in the middle of nowhere. Her arms stretched to the sky as she worshipped the light of day. Although it looked like a blissful moment, Morgan saw the look on Ella's face in this moment, and it was haunted.

"There's a story there." The words were whispered so low they tapped against the silence.

Morgan watched everything about Ella's body language change. Her shoulders sagged, her chest filled with a sorrowful breath as her eyes closed.

"Really?" Morgan asked.

"Yeah." Her finger touched the screen, tracing the outline of her outstretched arms. "That was my first fourteener." She swiped her cheek with the back of her hand.

"Fourteener?" The artist didn't understand the reference.

"My first hike to fourteen thousand feet." The words fell out in a disconnected pattern, as if Ella didn't want to say them. "It was almost six years ago that I went with a friend." She pulled her arms into her lap. "It was a dream of hers, to climb and hike together, and she's the one who actually took that picture."

Morgan stared at the screen for a long moment, listening to Ella take in and release a long breath. "I think it's a perfect visual summary of you." Morgan turned to look at Ella, who was wiping the cuff of her sleeve across her eye. She saw the glisten of tears but hesitated to ask more.

"That one was—" She paused to clear her throat and regain her voice. "That was our last hike together."

"Oh?" Morgan reached for Ella's free hand, bridging their fingers until she had a tight hold.

"She died."

"I'm so sorry."

Ella stared at the computer monitor, and it was clear to Morgan that the memory of their friendship was still fresh and the loss still raw. "She was an awkward, spindly woman with gangly long legs." Ella disappeared in remembering. "She had the loudest laugh in the history of laughter that accentuated her crooked toothy smile. She was unique, the very best of the best humans anyone would want to know. And she was my best friend." The declaration came out in a soul ripping whisper. And Morgan envied the devotion.

"Did you date?"

Ella shook her head. "She wasn't queer. She was just my Kay."

"I didn't mean to bring—"

Ella interrupted. "You didn't *do* anything. There's no way you could have known."

Morgan closed the browser window and turned off the work lamp. "Come with me."

She held a hand, and Ella took hold. Morgan guided her through the store and across the hall. The giant mouth of the elevator closed them inside. Under the glare of the dome light, Morgan had time to look at Ella's face. Her intention to confront the firefighter about her little deception had backfired into a trip down a trail of terrible memories. Hundreds of photographs, so many silly moments, and Morgan had to choose this one.

The elevator stopped, and Morgan took hold again as she led them to the living room. "Sit with me." She tugged Ella beside her.

"I'm not going to be good at this." She fidgeted.

Morgan didn't say a word. She expected more to come, but when nothing did, she broke the long, awkward silence. "You're very good at a lot of things, Ella Eastman."

A hitched whisper followed the head shake. "Not when it comes to Kay."

Morgan spent a lot of her life in a chair or at the counter. Rarely was she intentionally physical, like the gym rat sitting beside her. It was the first time she felt the full weight of a person with half her body fat, and if she wasn't more focused on comforting her pain, Morgan might have fallen over when Ella collapsed in her arms.

"Hey, it's all right. I've got you."

And that was the end of it. That was the last barrier holding back the tide of grief. Loss never ends; we only bury it. And from the shuddering and lack of words, Ella had been using a backhoe to hide from this pain.

Morgan pulled her legs up on the couch, glad that today's long skirt allowed for the ability to get that healing knee beside her. It hurt. She knew she'd need ice later, but Ella's body stretched across her lap, her head against her breast. All of Ella's hiccuped tears faded as she relaxed into Morgan's comforting touch.

Morgan held tight, aware of the scent of perspiration and smoke. This was the cologne of her firefighter. *Mine*, she thought. But could she honestly be?

<center>~~~~~~~~~~</center>

In moments like this, Morgan wished she had a sketch pad pinned to her arm. She couldn't remember a sight more stunning than the woman asleep in her lap. Where Morgan was soft in the body, Ella was hard. She was not ashamed to admit an attraction. It had been a long time since there was a woman in her home, aside from Beatrice.

Ella's arm came around to wrap herself closer to Morgan. She'd let her sleep, and later they would sort out Kay and the @Cinder_EllaE persona.

<center>~~~~~~~~~~</center>

"This is so embarrassing," Ella said into the pinstriped fabric smashed against her cheek.

Morgan's body shook as she laughed. "No, don't be embarrassed. It's fine. You're fine."

Ella was tangled against Morgan.

"Ahh, this just isn't me." She pushed away from Morgan's lap to sit beside her on the couch.

"I guess I would argue that it is you." Morgan stretched her legs.

Ella's elbows rested on her knees as she rubbed the haze of sleep from her eyes. "You caught me in a bit of a state. I haven't thought about her in a very long time."

"You said she died. How—" Morgan didn't have time to ask anything more when Ella interrupted.

"Uh, she. . . She took her life. She died by suicide."

Suicide. That wasn't what Morgan had expected to hear from the firefighter when she spoke about hiking and climbing. "Oh, I'm so sorry."

"Kay did it." She wrenched her fingers together, her voice holding a note of bitter anger. "Not one time did she ever

103

say she hurt that much. Not one time." She slapped her open hand on her knee. "She had a fucking amazing job. Perfect house, perfect guy, perfect life, but that wasn't enough. She had me, too, and somehow I wasn't enough either."

"I wish there was something I could do."

"Me, too." Ella pushed off the couch and walked toward the bedroom. "Do you mind if I use the bathroom?"

"Not at all."

She disappeared into the bedroom, and Morgan spent that time putting a kettle on to make hot water for tea. She didn't have much to drink in the house besides tea and the hot chocolate she kept for Beatrice. When Ella reappeared, her hair was pulled up tight into a sloppy bun, short curls tumbling out around her ears, and to Morgan, she was just about the most beautiful woman she had ever seen.

"So…" Ella drew out the word, and her whole demeanor reeked of uncertainty.

"Mm hmm." Morgan knew what was coming next.

"The Arsonist."

"Are we going to tackle that now?"

Ella stepped closer to the kitchen counter, her visibly stressed body on one side reflecting Morgan's rigid crossed-arm stance on the other. "There isn't anything I can say except that I'm sorry."

"Sorry for which part?" Morgan grabbed two mugs from the drying rack beside the sink and turned them over. "Would you like tea?"

"How about a shot of tequila? Or maybe some bourbon?"

Morgan's serious brown eyes looked at her.

"Tea would be fine."

Morgan dropped the bags on a saucer. "You know, I'm not really that mad about the confrontation in the vendor hall or even about the way you lured me to the Sage."

"Lured?" Ella was about to protest, but Morgan put a finger to her lips.

"Wait, let me finish. You had a lot of chances to come clean and you didn't. Why?"

Ella sighed. "I knew what I wanted to say. I stewed on it for weeks."

The kettle whistled on the stove, and the sound broke the tension. "But you didn't tell me."

"Because once I got to know you, I didn't want you to go away."

Morgan lifted the kettle, poured hot water in the cups, swirled it around, and dumped it out. She filled each cup and dropped in the bags. Her attention was on the process, intensely so, because she wanted to be mad, but after everything that had happened in the last hour, the anger was gone.

"So here's my deal." She reached across the counter to place a mug in front of Ella. "I like you. I like you quite a lot." She could tell Ella wanted to say something, so she lifted that petite, ink-stained finger again."I would like to spend more time together, but I won't be with you if this is who you are."

When Morgan dropped her finger, Ella said, "I promise that's not who I am."

"Good, so we have a deal?" She put her hand out to make a shake agreement, but Ella took hold, angled her body, turned her wrist over, and kissed the back of Morgan's hand.

Her eyes peeked up. "We have a deal."

CHAPTER 10

"Don't look at those." Ella tried to grab the phone from Morgan's hand.

The women sat close together on the couch, Ella's feet propped on the mosaic patterned footrest and Morgan's shoulder tucked in the curve of her arm. Tonight's featured event after a baked chicken dinner, left over from the station house lunch, was a deep dive into @Cinder_EllaE's social media stardom.

The firefighter was clever about posting experiences as a queer woman, as a queer firefighter, and opening up opportunities to empower strangers in her following. She was also enthusiastic about training with her bestie Marshy plum, which still needed an explanation. The posts about her workouts and after workout routines almost always included a shot of some part of Ella's body.

"I haven't even kissed you yet, but I've seen almost all of your body." Morgan's finger swiped the image, scrolling to the next on the page. "Two hundred and seventy-three thousand likes." She read a few of the follower comments. "How are you walking around the city without a bodyguard?" Morgan laughed as the muscular arm came around her to take the phone away, but she was holding her own.

"Damn, you're scrappy. You're stronger than you look." Ella stopped reaching for the phone and tucked her arms beneath Morgan. "Maybe you could be my bodyguard?" she joked as she pulled the smaller woman across her lap. "And if you'd like to remedy that kissing situation, I'm game."

Morgan held the phone up over her head, which was not far enough out of Ella's reach, but it brought their faces closer together. The laughter paused, the cellphone and their hands frozen in place above their heads.

Ella's breath caught as she glanced first at Morgan's lips, then back into her eyes. She felt the cue was there–a rapid heartbeat–heaving chest, but it might have been in her imagination.

"Ella." Her voice was breathy, and her pulse hammered hard.

"Yes?"

"I'd really like to kiss you?" Morgan bit at her bottom lip, nervous and incredibly aroused.

Ella closed her eyes. "I'd really like to be kissed by you."

The phone dropped, making a soft landing on the sofa cushion, but neither woman looked away. Morgan's hand moved to cup Ella's cheek, and when the firefighter opened her eyes again, heavy lidded grey eyes stared back.

There was surrender, lips touched, tentative and slight, feather soft one to the other, but Ella's heart felt bound to a strange, echoing outside force.

Ella's hand slid around the back of Morgan's neck, and she stroked a thumb against her chin. One of her long, calloused fingers touched Morgan's lips. "So beautiful," Ella whispered before bringing their lips together again.

Ella felt like a thirteen-year-old girl sneaking behind the softball bleachers. Like this was the first time she'd ever been kissed, but it was not. It was so very not. But if she had the choice, she would bottle this feeling and keep it forever. "Morgan, I—"

A fingertip touched her lips. "Shh, don't think anymore. Just keep kissing me."

~~~~~~~~~~

"I want you to come see my place." Ella smiled as the woman snuggled tighter into her embrace. Their first kiss had turned into a late night make-out session and neither wanted to let the other go.

Morgan's palm pressed against the firefighter's chest, over her heart so she could raise her eyes to see Ella's face. The stare was hypnotic, and Ella felt the attraction move from her heart to her toes.

"I would like to see your house."

Ella sat forward, shifting their bodies. "I have two nights on at the station starting tomorrow, but I want to cook dinner for you on my next off day."

"Yes, to all of it."

"That's very good." Ella felt a phone vibrate somewhere on the couch. She wasn't sure if it was hers or if it belonged to Morgan, but at this time of day, they probably needed to look at their messages.

"Should you check that?" Morgan whispered before kissing Ella.

Ella heard one sound, felt one feeling, and neither were prompted by the device on the couch. She moved away from soft lips, far enough to say, "Check what?"

Morgan's laugh was as delicate as her touch. "Nevermind, it doesn't matter."

~~~~~~~~~~

"Thursday works for me." Ella said as she printed her name in bold block letters, followed by her cell phone number, on the signup form.

"I'll take the time slot after yours." Lester bumped her shoulder to knock her sideways, but she was smarter than that maneuver and she didn't budge. "Who put this Cinder wall in my way?" He laughed at his own joke but noticed how solid she'd become.

"Smartass." She sidestepped his next bump, and he knocked into the wall. "Cold moves, Eastman."

"I hope you like that Santa suit, buddy." She snapped her fingers at him. Over the next few weeks, the station house rec room would transform into a photography studio. Ella liked the group of photographers and hoped that her idea for the shots for June would make the month a hit. She'd wear a crop top again, she knew, but she had something special in mind.

"I'm gonna crush December." He made a fierce tiger growl. "I'm gonna *Die Hard* that sucker!"

It was no surprise to the team hovering around the bulletin board that the ultra violent, macho mashup was Lester's favorite holiday movie. Last year's in-house survey for favorite film, centered on the Christmas-y vibe, included his write-in of *Die Hard.* And the ultimate result, winning by one vote was his favorite film. Word on the street was that Les cast the winning vote twice.

"I guess we'll see what the magicians of the calendar company let us do." Ella's shoulder fell against the wall, her lean an obvious display of pessimism.

"You're going to gay up June, aren't you?" The last two calendars had swimming pools and spattering fire hoses as a celebration of the month. Ella wanted more than anything to give the LGBTQIA community a firehouse rainbow shoot. She definitely had a plan to *gay* up June.

"You bet your ass I am. I channeled this month like a damn psychic."

He laughed as he walked toward the firehouse kitchen. "Help me make food, Cinder."

She stood on the opposite side of the countertop as Lester heaved all the vegetables for her to wash and cut. She plopped three peppers on the open flame to roast them. This was their way: team on the street, team in the kitchen. Ella rinsed the potatoes and got to chopping the onions while the skin on the peppers charred for Les's famous–legendary, as *he* called it–station house stew. It was not famous or legendary, but when he made it, there was never a spoonful to spare.

He slid a half dozen jars on the counter. "How's it going with the artist?" he asked as he twisted the top of the pepper mill, grinding it into the stainless steel bowl in front of him.

Ella's knife hand paused. She looked at him. "I think we're moving to the next phase." She scraped the charred skin away from the peppers, sliced them warm, and left the pile in a heap on the cutting board. She pushed it toward the center so Les could reach them when he was ready and began peeling the potatoes.

"Really slow playing this one, aren't you?" He didn't look up.

Ella smiled as she made a quick, tight sound. Not a sigh, but not a laugh, either. "I really like her, and I almost blew it, so, yeah, slow is how we're going. But there's no game."

"You told her about the convention?"

Ella shrugged. "I didn't tell her. She kinda found it on my social page."

"@Cinder_EllaE strikes again." He punched a fist at her, and she bumped it with the knuckles of her hand while clutching the peeling knife.

"I thought it was over, honestly." She continued peeling the potatoes. "But then she pulled up that fourteener picture, and I lost my shit." Her hands paused, but she couldn't look at Les. She knew if she did that, the tears would come.

It wasn't necessary for either of them to say her name. They had a long understanding that when the memories and anniversaries came, they got through them.

"You talked about her?" Lester stopped working.

Ella set the knife on the chopping board, the potato rolling toward her belly. "I told Morgan everything."

The smile on his face was a little like the reaction when grade schoolers passed notes in class. "So, you really do like this lady." It was a statement, not a question.

"Yeah, I really do."

"Finally!" Beatrice yelled across the gift shop.

Morgan was sitting at her desk, but the normally focused artist was resting her chin on her knuckles and staring at the half-finished sketch in front of her.

Morgan's body bounced in the seat, shaking everything on top of her desk. "Holy shit, B." She pushed her hand over her heart to calm the shock of her screech. "Finally, what?"

"You finally got to second base with the smokin' hot firefighter!" Her voice was loud enough for every pedestrian on the sidewalk to hear through the propped open door.

"Don't be such a child." Morgan kicked the desk to spin the chair around.

Beatrice's head bounced like a bobble doll. "But I'm right."

Morgan didn't even try to hide the grin on her face. "Maybe."

"Oh, did you take her to church?" B wriggled her eyebrows.

She tapped the pen on the desktop. Beatrice once referred to Morgan as "the nun on the run" because she liked women but wasn't always in a hurry to move a relationship beyond kissing and cuddles. Beatrice liked to tease, using the baseball metaphor, but when the mood hit, like it did now, the nun on the run all the way to church was better than a home run hit. "That's so gross. And no, we did not sleep together."

"But you want to sleep with her. I can see it."

The sigh was equal parts frustration with her friend and with herself. She didn't want to explain that maybe, just maybe, she'd like to spend the night with Ella and do more than cuddle.

"There's no rush. I'm not going anywhere, and neither is she. Plus she lives a dangerous life, and I don't know if I can be part of it."

"Does it bring up the …" She pointed at Morgan's legs. "With your grammy?"

Morgan thought for a moment. Ella knew about the fire and the scars and everything, but Ella ran toward danger for a living. That would always remind Morgan of her own past, and she might not be able to put that fear to rest.

"She's not like you and me, B." She turned her sketchpad over. "Regular people? They run from fires and car crashes and smoke and toxic goopy stuff. That's not her, though. She runs toward all of that and whatever else beeps on that box she wears."

"Toxic goopy stuff?" Beatrice repeated.

"That's what you're taking away from everything I just said?" She shook her head as she piled her art supplies into the wire mesh container.

"You should give her a chance."

Morgan tucked the supplies under her arm. "I'm doing that, just at my pace."

"Promise you won't run, my little nun."

She was halfway down the hall when she whispered, "I don't think I could even if I wanted to."

CHAPTER 11

"Calm down, woman," Ella scolded herself.

It was the third time she'd fluffed the pillows on the couch and the fourth time she'd peeked through the front door window. She was nervous, more than she'd been about every other date they'd had the last few months. Morgan was about to see how the firefighter lived. How overstuffed the second bedroom was with costumes and materials to build replicas of her favorite weapons, and how practically impractical she was at heart.

Ella was so wrapped up in checking and double checking the food in the oven, she didn't hear the soft tapping on the door. She jumped when the noise became a thump. She wasn't expecting anyone but Morgan. The security chain rattled against the frame as she opened the door. The petite woman stood there, the green tips of her hair faded away into the clump of a bun tied on her head.

Ella stood, frozen to the spot, her heart hammering at the sight of this woman. Grey eyes blinked once and then twice before Morgan said, "You were expecting me, right?"

"Oh, uh, yeah."

"Would it be okay if I came inside?" She raised her eyebrow and pointed inside the cottage.

"Damn, yes." She sidestepped so Morgan could enter. "I'm sorry. You just look so amazing, and I got…" She stopped talking.

Morgan raised her hand to touch Ella's cheek. "It's alright. I kinda feel the same way." Before they shared another word, she stretched on her toes to kiss the firefighter.

Ella's hands fell to Morgan's waist as she bent closer, and the kiss, although featherlight, was the perfect greeting.

"Hi," she said.

Ella could barely form a word. "Hi."

She clenched her fingers as she closed the door with her elbow, trying to reel in her anxiety. This was Morgan, and she liked Ella, and she was going to like the cottage Ella called home.

"So this is my place." She waved around the entry. "Living room." She pointed to the love seat and table. "Kitchen." She walked to the other side of the love seat. "And the dining room."

Her hand rested on the two-person round table pushed against the wall. It was nothing like the high ceilings of Morgan's loft, but it was hers and just enough for a person who was away more than she was at home.

She reached for the bag on Morgan's shoulder. "Let's put this here, and I can show you the rest of the place." She dropped Morgan's things on the table and led her down the narrow hall. "This is my studio, nothing like yours, but I make all of my costume pieces here."

Morgan stepped past Ella and took her time surveying the room. The sewing table had an old machine built into the base. It was well kept, but most of the lettering and embossed features had worn away. Her fingers ran across the fabric, folded and piled on a shelf. The room was full but organized, and Ella was proud she'd made such a great space to create.

"This must be your favorite place to work," Morgan said.

"I love it in here." Ella held out her hand, leading the woman to the last room in the house. "And when I'm not at the station, this is where I sleep."

Morgan stood in the doorway, eyeing the bedspread on Ella's queen-sized bed.

Ella noticed the curious expression. "Not what you expected?"

"Not at all."

"You should know by now that I'm not a complex person, Morgan. I may like to dress up and make believe, but this is the real me." She waved at the bedroom.

"I like the real you."

"Yeah?"

Morgan smiled. "Yeah."

The timer in the kitchen interrupted the conversation. "That would be dinner."

Morgan followed her into the kitchen and sat at the small table while Ella cooked. Out of the corner of her eye, Ella watched her remove the sketch pad from her bag and make a few quick strokes on the page.

"What are you working on?" Ella asked as she removed two plates from the cabinet.

"I got this idea today while I was looking at your calendar outfit from last year." She turned back a few pages in her notebook.

"Uugh, you had to remind me." She covered her face and laughed. "Not my favorite moment?"

"I think it's adorable. You were going for adorable, right?" She looked up with the most playful smile Ella could remember from this woman.

"Absolutely going for fluffy and adorable."

Morgan walked to the counter and held up her sketchpad. "I started with your piece because I knew the most about you."

Ella took hold of the pad and stared for the longest time. She didn't say a word as she looked down at the lightly shaded colored pencil drawing.

Morgan's hands trembled as she turned the page. "There are stats for you. I kinda made them up because I don't know what's important. But I thought you could help, and maybe I could talk to the rest of the crew, the January through November people for the backsides." She said it all in one nervous breath.

"You made firehouse trading cards?"

"I thought you could sell them with the calendars. Maybe get kids involved, too?"

Ella's hip fell against the counter as she turned the pages in the sketchbook. "Lester! Oh, this one is so good. Morgan, you're an extraordinary artist."

"So you like them?"

"Like is hardly the best way to describe it." She held a hand out to the artist and wrapped her in a hug. Morgan turned in the embrace to take the sketches back.

Ella held her closer. "I want you to come with me to the station tomorrow. Lester organizes most of the fundraisers, and he should see these."

"On your day off?"

She shrugged. "It'll be just a short visit, and I'm sure they'll be happy to put a face with the name."

"Remember that I met Lester."

"I remember. But he didn't see your work, and I think he should."

"I can ask Beatrice to watch the shop."

"So you'll go with me?" Ella embraced her.

"I'll go with you," Morgan said as her belly made a loud, rumbly sound.

"Are you hungry?" Ella teased.

"Famished, can't you hear?" Morgan stepped back to the table. "Would you like some help?"

Ella passed her the cutlery and napkins. "Put these out and then come back for a plate."

The meal was simple: baked fish, seasoned rice, and French cut style green beans. It wasn't her most popular, but she wanted their night to run late, and full bellies made for tired company.

"Glass of wine?"

"Just a little. I have to drive."

Ella poured a small amount in a glass but didn't pour one for herself.

"None for you?"

Ella shrugged her shoulder as she sat down beside Morgan. "I don't really drink. Maybe done it three or four times."

"I remember the first night at the Sage you only had seltzer." There was a question on her face, but she didn't ask it.

"I don't have a problem with alcohol, if that's what you're wondering."

Morgan looked at her, her eyes glued to Ella's lips. "I was wondering, but I guess I thought it was related to what you see out there." She pointed at the duffle bag with the fire department logo on it.

Ella set her fork on the plate, took a sip of her water, and said, "Not to get too serious, but it's related in a way. A drunk driver killed both of my parents"

Morgan's hand stretched across the table. "Why do I keep doing this? Oh, Ella, I'm so sorry."

"It's okay, Morgan." Their fingers laced together, and Ella's clenched as she said, "I was behind my mother, strapped into a car seat safe and sound. I don't really remember much." She pulled back her curls to tuck them over her right ear. "This is the only evidence I was there." The scar was faint after almost twenty-five years. "Remember what I said about scars? We all have some, and we all wear them differently."

Morgan gave her a small smile and squeezed her hand.

~~~~~~~~~~~~~~~~

The dishes from dinner soaked in soapy water in the sink. The untouched glass of wine was still on the table. Ella adjusted her position on the couch so her legs stretched out with Morgan tucked in between them.

Morgan raised her palm, which fit perfectly in the warmth of Ella's calloused hands. "Your hands are an interesting subject."

Ella's chest vibrated from the brief laugh. "Subject for what, exactly?"

"For my sketchbook, of course."

Ella considered the lens Morgan viewed the world through. "If I could draw, I'd say your hands are more interesting than mine. You have ink." She touched the stain on her middle finger. "Probably from the lines on that Arsonist piece. Just a guess."

"Mm hmm. Very good."

"And this right here." She rotated the pointer finger to get a view of the tip. "This is nervous biting."

"Very nervous biting."

Ella kissed the fingertip. "Nervous because of tonight?" Their hands steepled together.

"Yes, because of this." She motioned to their position on the couch. Her heart was beating so hard that Ella could feel it in her own chest.

"Nothing will happen tonight, Morgan."

The smaller woman let out a deep breath. "I'm not good at everything that comes after holding hands."

"You are attracted to women?" Ella asked.

Morgan nodded.

"I've only ever been with women, but I'm not always interested in sex," Ella told her. "You're not going to be a notch
~~~~~~~~~~~~~~~~

on my bedpost. Just because I look a certain way doesn't mean that's how I am."

"But you're attracted to me?" Morgan's cheeks flushed.

Ella nodded with a huge smile. Their bodies tight in this embrace were nearly perfection and she felt the heat travel down her neck and chest.

"That's very good because I am very attracted to you, Ella Eastman." The confession was whispered so quietly that the firefighter almost didn't hear her.

"You understand that you're safe with me?"

Morgan relaxed against Ella, her eyes shut tight. "I have never felt so safe with anyone before. Never, ever."

She turned her body until she could slip an arm beneath Ella. They laid there for the longest time, listening to the sound of each other's breath. Ella felt Morgan's body relax along the length of hers.

They were in the same position when Ella woke a few hours later. Nothing about the energy in the room had changed.

"It's getting so late," Ella said, and Morgan was quick to respond.

"I should probably go, but…"

"But?" Ella prompted.

Morgan took a deep breath, then smiled. "But I don't want to."

It was Ella's turn to smile, but she was also nervous. Her voice caught in her throat a bit as she asked, "How would you feel about staying together for the night?"

Every part of her wanted to stay. The house felt like a home. The body tight behind her felt like safety and the featherlight kisses to the top of her head felt like adoration. Why would she ever want to leave? Morgan's body shifted when Ella took a deep breath.

"I w-would like to st-stay with y-you," she stammered out, voice unsteady. There were hundreds of thoughts rattling around inside Morgan's brain about sleeping with this attractive woman. Her palms were sweaty, and her hands trembled as she tried to pull them to her chest.

Ella must've felt Morgan's body tense because she said, "We don't have to do anything but hold each other and sleep. It feels good just to be near you, and it has nothing to do with sex."

Morgan hitched her hip to turn toward Ella so she could see her face. "You don't want to have sex?" For most of the evening, Morgan had played out all the scenarios in her head: the tour of the house that stopped at the bedroom, the glass of wine poured only for her, the delicious meal light enough for a late night together, and the enthusiastic interest in Morgan's art. All of it felt scripted with an obvious final scene: sex.

"Being with you isn't really about sex."

Morgan's face screwed into an expression of total disbelief. "*Not about sex*" was something she said in her head all the time. "You're saying that if I stay with you, we can do this." She waved at their fully clothed positions. "Just hold each other and feel safe."

"Nothing else."

Morgan shimmied against Ella, their bodies connecting between their shoulders and toes. "I don't have anything to sleep in," she said against Ella's chest.

"I'll give you something of mine."

Morgan laughed. "You still have clothes from middle school?" Arms tightened around her as she felt the firefighter chortle.

"Would you feel comfortable in…" She hesitated and then redirected the question. "I'll find something for you. Don't worry."

Ella disappeared into the bedroom a few minutes later, and Morgan stood at the sink, washing dishes from their meal. As she stared at the foam of soap bubbles in the water, she felt a sense of calm. She was here, safe and feeling no pressure to be something she was not. She was lost in thought when she felt a hand at the small of her back.

"I've got these." Ella held up a pair of sweatpants. The extended length made Morgan laugh.

"They're about a foot too long. I'll strangle myself in my sleep."

They both laughed, and Ella held up the pair of scissors she'd brought out of the spare room. "Hold these at your waist."

Morgan dried her soap covered hands and pinched the sweatpants near each of her hipbones.

"Don't move." Ella pressed the fabric, with the faintest touch, against Morgan's shin, and snipped a mark where she would cut them off. She carried the pants to the table, laid them out flat, and chopped off more than eight inches from each leg.

"Clever," Morgan said as she returned to the sink of dishes.

"You do know what it means when a lesbian cuts her pants for you?" Ella joked.

Morgan shook her head as she turned around. "I'm not sure I've read that stipulation in the handbook."

"Oh, it's there. I even think it's highlighted and in bold." Ella teased.

"What's it say?"

Ella smiled as she trimmed the seam's edge. "It means you're going to have to make sure that they aren't lonely."

"The pants or the person who cut them?" Morgan asked, feeling playful in what could be an awkward moment.

"Good call. And just to be sure, maybe take care of both."

"I think I can handle both."

Ella raised a questioning brow. "Can you?"

"Easy as pie. I was more concerned that the pants came with a Uhaul attached to a Subaru."

Ella's laugh was loud as she took the scrap pieces and the scissors back into the spare room. "You're all set. Sleeping bottoms and a sleeping shirt." She set the faded fire department t-shirt on top of the pants.

"What size is that?" Morgan giggled at the absurdity of their physical size differences.

"It's old, probably a large."

"Large."

Ella smiled. "I can't do much about that one."

"It's cute." She dried her hands on the towel. "Are we going to bed or back to the couch?"

Ella looked at her watch. "Do you usually stay up past eleven?"

"I stay up based on the next day's schedule, and since my rage rooms are all ready to go, my morning will be pretty easy."

"So you're…"

Morgan picked up the cut-off sweatpants and the faded shirt. "Let's go to bed."

Ella held her hand as she walked backward down the hallway. She stopped in front of the bathroom. "You can have this first. I'll change in there." She pointed toward the bedroom.

"Thank you." Morgan stepped inside and closed the door.

She was really going to do this. She was going to climb into bed with an attractive woman who wouldn't paw at her or try to convince her that her sexuality was invalid or just some anxious nerves. If Morgan could see Ella now, she'd find it funny that their actions were almost mirrored images: shirts and bras off, sleep shirts on, socks and jeans off, sleep pants on.

Morgan laughed as she tugged the drawstring tight, and absurd tangled loops dangled near her thigh. The outfit made her feel all of her five foot four inches, but the jagged edges at her ankles made her feel adored. She peeked her head out into the hall. "Can I use some toothpaste?"

"In the cabinet over the sink, and there are floss sticks in the metal tin," Ella said.

Morgan opened the mirrored door and removed the tube of whitening paste, along with a single flossing stick. She took that moment to contemplate Ella's very white teeth. The rest of the cabinet was typical with face cream and pimple gel. Two containers of multivitamins and some protein supplements. Feeling a touch nosy, she squeezed a dab of toothpaste on her fingertip and did her best job of brushing away tonight's dinner.

A few minutes later, she met Ella in the hallway. "Thank you for the paste."

"If I'd known, I would have had a toothbrush for you, too."

Morgan brushed her hand as she walked by. "Somehow, I believe you would have." She stretched on her tiptoes to kiss her cheek. "You're very sweet."

Ella turned toward the bathroom, her fingertips light against the remnants of the kiss.

~~~~~~~~~

"You're very warm." Morgan said as Ella spooned in behind her.

"I hope that's a good thing."

Morgan's feet came up to touch Ella's shins.
~~~~~~~~~

"Oh, and you would be the complete opposite." She pulled Morgan closer.

"It's a circulation thing. I know my feet are cold, but I also have nerve damage that prevents me from really feeling it."

"Peripheral neuropathy?" Ella whispered.

Of course she would know about it, Morgan thought.

"Do you usually wear socks in bed?"

Morgan smiled and, not for the first time, thought this woman was too good to be true. "Pretty much without fail."

"You should always be the most comfortable, Morgan, especially with me." Ella rolled away and off the bed. She opened the second drawer of her dresser and pulled out a balled pair of padded socks. "Come here," she said, and Morgan sat up, the blanket pooling around her hips. "Feet please." Ella popped the socks apart and opened the cuff wide enough.

Morgan knew Ella saw the scars on her toes and up her ankles, but her expression never changed. Ella was an incredible woman.

"You realize it should be me putting the slipper onto your foot, Cinder Ella?"

The smile that followed was the most perfect expression Morgan had witnessed all evening.

"Next time," Ella said as wriggly toes slipped one after the other inside the heavy socks.

"I'm going to remember you said that." She pulled her feet back under the blanket, curled onto her side and waited for muscled arms to come under her neck and over her hip. This was definitely felt better than any fairy tale.

CHAPTER 12

Every thought was about a collection of feelings: the tingly sensation of a head resting on her bicep, leaving numbness in her fingers, a contoured ass snugged tight into her abdominals creating an intimate warmth, delicate fingers clamped to calloused hands resting over a steady beating heart. A woman, deep in sleep, intimately woven to her so much so that she could not discern where one started and the other might end.

She never wanted to move from this bed, not ever. In this waking moment, she understood with clarity that this must be what love feels like.

Morgan turned, letting out a mouselike squeak as she nuzzled into Ella's chest.

Ella's breath hitched, and with exercised control, it released over the top of Morgan's loose hair. She rolled to her back, finding relief from the hand tingles, but getting a new sensation from this sprite of a woman's leg hooking over her hip.

This could definitely be love.

~~~~~~~~~

Ella woke a few hours later as sunlight peeked through the edge of the curtain. Her watch read seven-fifteen and her body ached to rise and race to the gym. There was one thing–person, really–in the way of everything she'd known as routine: Morgan Hail.

"Your muscles just got all hard and tense." Morgan's head turned as she spoke against Ella's shoulder.

"Just waking up." Her back arched, and the petite person in her arms moved with her.

"And?"

She scooted toward the headboard to rest against it. "Mornings at home are a bit like flying on autopilot."

Morgan moved beside her, folding her pillow in half for added support. "Cuddling with me is probably not in that routine, huh?"

Ella pretended to scroll through an imaginary list in her palm. "Nope, cuddling is rarely on the list." She pretended to lick the point of her invisible pen. "But I'm adding it now."

Morgan's hand rested in her lap, the blanket bunched around her waist. "I don't know how to thank you for last night."

"I think you just did." Her fingers traveled down Morgan's palm until their hands tangled together. "It's more than that, though. Few people understand what we *didn't* do last night."

Ella shrugged. "There's something between us, and it feels different to me, so, yeah, I want to keep that safe. Keep *you* safe."

"I feel it too, and if it's okay, I want to be with you a lot more."
~~~~~~~~~

"I'd like that." The kiss was the perfect seal to their agreement.

Morgan's head rested against the bed. "So, tell me, where would you be right now?"

Ella held up her watch. "In the gym with Marsh."

"Until when?"

"Since we have an appointment at the station house, right until then."

Morgan lumped her feet over the side of the bed and stood. "I'm going to get dressed, put myself together, and go home."

"Don't go yet." Ella fell over, trying to grab the woman's hand. "Stay longer."

Morgan picked up her clothes and stepped wide around the bed to avoid Ella's quick hands. "I'm getting dressed, and you should, too, if you want to walk me to my car." She disappeared into the hallway.

"No fair!" Ella said to the empty room. As much as she wanted to stay in bed, Morgan was making a good choice for both of them.

The bell over the door to the gift shop jingled as she pushed it open. She was doing her very best to avoid Beatrice by not using the service entrance where she thought her business partner would be at this time of the day. She misjudged her friend's excitement.

"Is that Morgan Hail doing the walk of shame?" Her head popped up from behind the pile of boxes.

"There is no shame in my walk." She plunked her bag on the desk. "I'm pleased as can be about coming home after an amazing evening with an amazing woman."

"You spent the night with the hot fire—fighter—." She drew out the last two words.

"Ella. Her name is Ella, and she's not just a hot firefighter." She dropped into the chair.

"How was she?"

Morgan's brow scrunched, disapproving of the question. "How was she what?"

"Oh, why do you play me like this? I know you're not celibate."

Morgan picked up her bag and walked toward the elevator. "You'll never get me to kiss and tell."

"Morg, you can't just leave me with nothing." Beatrice folded her hands together, making her most desperate plea.

"She's probably the best…" She hesitated, drawing out the suspense. "…cuddler I've ever had in my entire life."

"Cuddles?" Beatrice yelled, but it was too late. Morgan was already lifting to the second floor.

~~~~~~~~~~

"I'm going to take a quick shower and I'll be over to pick you up," Ella said. "You aren't busy, are you?"

"Oh, I'm busy alright. Beatrice has been nagging me for hours to give her details about our date last night."

Morgan heard a car door close and a key turn in the ignition as Ella said, "Really?"

"Oh yes, she's going on and on about how hot you are and how you must have knocked my socks off."

Ella laughed. "It was actually the opposite, but she never needs to know."

"Prepare yourself for the best friend grilling of your life."

"Thanks for the warning."

Morgan smiled when she heard the rumble of Charlene's engine. Secretly, she loved that car.

"I'll see you in a few minutes." Ella ended the call.

Morgan stared at Beatrice, then glanced at the clock. It was a quick trip to R.A.T.S. Rage Room from Ella's place, and she readied herself for whatever Beatrice felt she needed to do to protect her best friend.

~~~~~~~~~~

"And you've never been married?"

Beatrice had a list of questions scribbled on a piece of paper that had obviously been ripped from a notebook. The frayed edge pieces fell, making Morgan a little uncomfortable as the woman walked in circles around Ella where she sat in the waiting room chair. The entire scene was endearing, and Morgan was glad Beatrice was the kind of friend who would take on this Amazonian woman.

"Longest relationship was two years," Ella replied with a cool demeanor. "We exchanged no vows."

"Two years." Beatrice tapped the pencil eraser to her lip, scribbled a note on the paper and asked. "Why'd you split?"

"Hey, uh no!" Morgan made a T with her hands. "Time out, not appropriate to ask."

"It's fine, Morgan. I have nothing to hide."

"I'll be the judge of that," Beatrice said as she leaned closer. "You were going to say?"

"My life doesn't always fit into a neat schedule." She shrugged. "She didn't want to be alone, and sometimes I wanted my alone time."

"Are you planning to dump my best friend?"

If Beatrice had a bright spotlight, Morgan was sure it would be shining in Ella's face. "B, stop it right now." Morgan stepped in front of Ella, blocking Beatrice with her entire body. "I think she knows that you're here to be my attack dog."

"More like a ferocious lion. Or a bear." Beatrice held up her hands, making clawing gestures at the firefighter.

"I have a black belt, so you might want to be careful," Ella warned and made her best attempt at clenched fighting hands.

"That's such a lie," Beatrice said and flopped in the chair, the paper and pencil dropping to her lap.

Ella's long legs kicked out, crossing at the ankles in the most relaxed position she'd displayed since arriving to pick up Morgan. "Not a lie. Kenpo for self defense. Fourteen years of muscle memory, so be warned, the body never forgets."

"So you're gonna kick my ass?" Beatrice slapped the paper list against her thigh. "No fair, I'm supposed to get all tough girl, large with the butch, and make *you* feel uncomfortable."

"She's a firefighter, B." Morgan held her hand out to Ella. "She eats uncomfortable for breakfast."

Ella's cheeks pressed into a smile when Beatrice crossed her arms with a stern foot stomp.

"You can pout at the front desk," Morgan told her. "We've got a small group at two."

"Yeah, yeah. I've got it covered."

"Large with the butch, really?" Morgan scolded, giving her friend the sternest scrunched brow.

"Just looking out for my bestie." Beatrice blew a kiss.

Morgan followed Ella toward the door, and the firefighter took the shoulder bag, pretending its weight was a burden. "You been painting on rocks?" she teased.

"Just bringing the best of my best," Morgan said.

The bell jingled once and jingled again, and Morgan hoped that Beatrice could see that Ella and Morgan were a perfect fit.

~~~~~~~~~~

"For the record, I prefer eggs over uncomfortable, for breakfast," Ella said as she opened the passenger door for Morgan and walked around to the driver's side.

"It was stupid, I know, but she can really be nosy and go way too far."

Ella put the key in the ignition. "You might want to prepare yourself for Lester and the rest of the team."

"Will it be as bad as B?"

"Nah." Ella pumped the gas peddle a few times before starting the car. "They're a thousand times worse."

~~~~~~~~~~

"You did these?" Phil Brentwood, the lieutenant of the department and perhaps the most important person to impress for this project, sat flipping pages back and forth in Morgan's sketchbook.

"I did." She opened the file on her tablet to share some of her digital work.

"I've seen these," Lester said as the portfolio landed on the table in front of him. "Eastman, you have this one, don't you?" He held up the image of The Arsonist.

Ella nodded. "I have the postcard. It's in my locker."

Morgan studied the woman for a moment. She didn't remember selling it to Ella, but as she ran through her convention patrons, she remembered. *Very sneaky, Ella,* she thought. She exchanged a knowing glance with Ella, who blushed a little.

"So you want to do these for all of us?" Phil pointed to the rest of the firefighters in the lounge.

"I'd like to." Morgan reached for the folder in her bag. "I made a form. It has all the questions for your statistics that go on the back." She left the stack on the table. "If I get a form, I'll make you a card."

"There's no price on here." Lester flipped the page over. "We're not going to let you do this for free."

Morgan switched to her tablet. "My fees for commissions are hourly."

"How many hours will each card take?" Phil asked.

"Six at most if you do a great job with the forms and I have access to the photographer's files."

Lester took charge of the impromptu proposal meeting. "I have no idea what your hourly rate is, but we will contract you the same way we do the photographer." He held up Ella's trading card sample. "These are going to sell and they'll be great for public relations."

"That's what I thought!" Ella's excitement was impossible to hide.

"Twelve months, twelve firefighters." Lester tapped the papers in front of him. "The calendar printing usually takes three months. If we get the photos to you at the same time, can you make that schedule work?"

"That's a week per card," she said, doing the math in her head. "Final project piece would be two by three inch trading size, right?"

Lester nodded.

"Absolutely possible."

"Write up a contract, miss, and we'll make this happen." Lester held a hand to her and Morgan gave it a quick shake. "Now that we've settled that, how would you like to see where our Cinder works?" He held his elbow to her and Morgan hooked her hand through.

"I think I'd like that very much."

CHAPTER 13

After the tour, Ella met Morgan on the sidewalk where she parked the car, then took the messenger bag from Morgan to toss it over her broad shoulder. She didn't give it a thought; she wanted to lighten Morgan's load and also position their bodies closer when they walked. Their tour of the station was more involved than Ella had expected, but Morgan had seemed to enjoy every minute. "Is he always such a flirt?"

"Maybe a bit. I think he was trying to do what B did, but with a little more tact." She held her hand out, and Morgan's slid into it. "He wasn't too much, was he?" She tugged their bodies together.

"Not at all, but I didn't have a black belt to scare him off."

Ella laughed. "You could. I can teach you." Her arm swept up Morgan's back and hitched over her shoulder as she positioned herself between Morgan and the street.

"Maybe I'll keep you around, instead." Morgan grinned.

They were cute walking side by side, and the longer they were together, the less all of their differences mattered.

"I like the sound of that."

"Was that your stomach?" Morgan asked, trying to hide the laugh at the outrageous sound coming from Ella's belly.

"I definitely could eat." The bell over the door jingled, and Beatrice popped out from behind a clothing rack.

"I didn't call for an emergency." She threw her forearms over the hanging shirts. "You keep bringing that hot—"

Morgan shot forward and shoved her hand over Beatrice's mouth. "That's about enough out of you and this smart mouth." Morgan turned to acknowledge the laughter coming from the door. "Don't encourage her." She pointed at Ella with the most intimidating stare she could muster.

"So feisty." Ella's hands went up in surrender as she walked over to set Morgan's bag on the desk.

"You haven't seen feisty yet." Morgan turned back to Beatrice. "You! Behave yourself!" She said each word with a finger point, then dropped her hand. "Nothing from you." She made a zipping motion over her mouth.

"But every time she comes in it gets hot in h—"

Morgan looked at Ella. "Maybe those karate lessons aren't such a bad idea."

"Maybe, but your friend seems scrappy." Ella made her best shuffle step with a few quick jabs, but the maneuver was more delicious than intimidating.

"See," Beatrice said in her defense. "So fucking hot."

Morgan grabbed Ella by the wrist and dragged her toward the elevator.

"Someone named Morgan Hail needs to sit in the shop!" Beatrice yelled.

No words were exchanged as the sound of the elevator doors lifted and lowered and the two women disappeared to the second floor.

~~~~~~~~~~

"Who taught you how to cook?" Ella scooped the last bite of casserole onto her fork.

Morgan stood at the counter, holding the spatula over the baking dish. "More?" she asked, and Ella raised a hand in surrender.

"It's amazing, but I can't eat another bite." She set her fork on the plate.

"Um, cooking. I guess I learned from myself, really." She cut the remaining noodle and chicken combination into Ella-sized pieces and put them into containers.

"This was so good." She carried the plate to the kitchen and plunged it into the soapy water. Without hesitation, she finished washing everything.

"True confession." She didn't wait for Ella to respond. "That came from a magazine."

Ella took the dish from her hand. "I want to make it for the team. They'd go nuts."

The conversation continued as they finished washing and cleaning the kitchen. "I should get back down there." Morgan pointed at the floor. "Time to go to work." She draped the towel over the handle of the oven. "She's got her real time gig, too."

"Harsh light of day and all that." Ella held a hand toward Morgan. "Come on, I'll stop distracting you."

Strong hands raised the elevator door, and they stepped inside. "Will you come back tonight?"

"Since you asked, I'd love to."

Morgan smiled as the elevator doors opened. "Bring something to sleep in, because as cute as I looked in your clothes, I can't reciprocate."
~~~~~~~~~~

"Got it." Ella winked.

"And for the record…" Morgan paused.

"Uh huh?"

"That was an open invitation for you to come back and stay."

Ella kissed her forehead. "Duly noted."

~~~~~~~~~~

"Are you nervous about today?" Morgan sat on the bed in Ella's cottage, her feet kicking off the side. It was early, just at the peak of sunrise, but they'd been awake for hours. Ella's normally restful slumber was replaced with endless hip hitches and arm adjustments. She stood in front of the closet, a rainbow patterned sports bra covering her breasts.

"It's just doing a pride theme. Maybe they won't like it." She tucked a shirt and strips of rainbow striped fabric into her duffle bag. "It's supposed to be for charity."

"The photographers went over it, didn't they?" Morgan asked, and it was obvious to Ella that Morgan wasn't distracted as she dressed.

"They did."

Morgan began ticking off each of her comments with her fingers. "And the department chief gave it the thumbs up?"

"He did."

She held the third finger up, bending it for emphasis. "Your team loves the idea?"

Ella smiled. Their support was confirmation that they weren't only coworkers, but a solid supportive chosen family. "They do."

"And you've done this calendar three times already." She winked at her. "Really well, if my observations matter."

"I have, and they do." She stepped in between Morgan's legs and bent down for a kiss. "All of those things are great, but I still have to get half naked and be sexy."
~~~~~~~~~~

She made the least sexy pose. She would never see herself as the rest of the world did. This calendar was about objectifying what Ella held dear: her hard work and commitment to being the best firefighter out there.

Morgan didn't laugh. "You're going to be amazing, El." Cold hands grasped Ella's hips.

She stared at Morgan, an eyebrow raised in question. "El?" she repeated.

"Yeah, I thought it seemed—"

"It seems absolutely perfect when it comes from your lips." She kissed her again and stepped back to finish loading her bag with rainbow patterned clothing options.

"How many pictures will they take?" Morgan asked.

Ella zipped the bag and tossed it toward the bedroom door. "Hundreds, maybe thousands, I guess. It seems like the camera clicks nonstop for three hours."

"That's a lot of pictures. I'm glad they're only sending me three or four."

"Can you believe there are thousands of pictures of this?" She waved up and down her torso.

Morgan swallowed hard. "I think I changed my mind."

Ella's head popped through the fire department t-shirt, "About?"

"Watching the photo shoot."

Ella stepped against the bed, hands on Morgan's shoulders, and pushed her down. Their faces were inches apart as Ella's body hovered, muscles flexing. "You have to be there."

Morgan swallowed hard.

Ella wondered as her heart hammered in her chest if Morgan's heart did, too.

"I might not be able to stand there, watching you, and not feel things."

"You don't have to hide your desire, Morgan. I'm with you for all of it." Their kiss was tender. "Your heart. It's beating so hard." Ella held her body up with one hand as she placed her palm over Morgan's chest.

"I…" She couldn't make words come out of her mouth. "I think—."

Ella stared at the woman, studying the way her eyes dilated, huge pupils hiding the grey hue she adored. "I love you, too, Morgan."

After the heat of their kiss and the proclamation of love, Morgan wanted to be with Ella. It had nothing to do with possessive behavior or lustful thoughts; it had everything to do with being in love. They held hands in the car, and Ella raced around to open the door after they parked.

Morgan witnessed it, felt it, understood exactly how Ella was selfless.

"So it's not like when they come to film. You can ask questions and even make suggestions. Lester did it a lot last year, and I think the last shot of my fuzzy crop top was his idea."

"He'll be here, too?"

"With his smart-ass on in all that Santa suit glory."

Morgan sighed. "At least I'll have someone to talk to."

Ella held the door open. "You might regret saying that."

"Cinder!" Lester's call was loud, and when he noticed Morgan, he kicked it up a notch. "You brought that gorgeous woman of yours."

Yours, Morgan thought. She'd said the *L* word, kind of, and that meant something about togetherness and couple-y-ness. What else could it mean?

"Hi, Lester." Morgan gave a light, bashful wave.

"Cinder, your lady is so adorable."

"She has a name, you know." Ella squeezed her hand before letting it go.

"Morgan, I'm just playin'. We're all glad to have you." He waved around the ambulance bay. "Rigs are out front getting a shine from the Probie." He hitched a thumb toward the side of the building. "Photogs are setting up in there." He waved at the curtained cubical.

"What's a 'probie'?" she whispered to Ella.

She set her duffle bag on the table. "Probationary candidate. Wilson's been here six months. He's a dedicated but inexperienced student, a quick study and my second Probie."

"So you're a mentor?"

"We all are, but I also listen when he wants to quit and encourage him when he fails."

Morgan didn't want to be nosy, but she was curious about the steps to become a firefighter. "I suppose that happens a lot?"

"Less than you'd think. Once they get in here, they've been through some mental and physical challenges in school." Ella looked at the cases on the floor. "Photographer is in here?"

As two people walked into the bay, Lester winked and said, "Getting ready to set up for you, sexy thang."

"Shut it, Soot-boy." She walked away from Morgan and Lester to spend a few minutes talking to the photographer and their apprentice.

"She's nervous, but she'll never admit it," he said as they took a seat just outside of the area designated for the shoot.

Morgan thought about the conversation in Ella's bedroom and her confession. Something in that level of honesty made her feel appreciated more than she had before.

"She's got a duffle bag full of rainbows," Morgan shared.

He threw his arm over the back of her chair. "That's a big deal."

"Celebrating Pride Month?"

"That." His head tipped toward the Captain's office. "And having the support of the higher ups."

They sat for a moment, and Morgan could sense he had something else to say.

"Uh," he began slowly, "has she talked much about Kay?"

Morgan's shoulders stiffened because Kay was practically off-limits, and she wasn't sure she should say anything about what little she knew.

"It's okay." He nodded at Ella. She'd walked out of the locker room wearing her turnouts but was still far enough away that she couldn't hear them. "I know you know about her, but the anniversary is coming up. She won't say anything, but when she disappears, that's the reason why."

"Disappears?" Morgan asked, and she didn't try to hide her concern in the question.

"It's how she deals," he said.

"What day?" Morgan asked. She looked at Ella and then back at him. "When?"

"Next Tuesday, but she'll get very quiet on Sunday."

"What should I do?" The exchange felt like a betrayal, like sharing a secret, but she knew he wanted her to understand his best friend.

"There's nothing you can do. Just be there for her."

Morgan watched the coat drop over Ella's shoulder, revealing the rainbow stripes on her suspenders. Lester gave a whistle and a few claps, and Ella responded with two middle fingers.

"I'll be there," Morgan said, her eyes never leaving the beautiful woman in front of her.

For the next two hours, Morgan watched and sketched and watched a bit more. There were ladders and hoses and little rainbow flags painted on Ella's skin. Morgan's favorite pose was of Ella yoking a sledge hammer with her helmet tipped toward the floor. Even with that chiseled face hidden, every inch of her torso glistened with oil, aside from the strategically placed rainbow bikini top.

Morgan did her best to hide her attraction, but when Ella tipped her helmet up, their eyes met, and the heat that passed between them was blazing. She watched Ella push off the wall, lay the sledgehammer on the bench, and hug the photographer.

Lester's arm fell off the chair. "I guess that's my cue to get into my Santa suit."

"Thanks for the company." Morgan gave him a quick wave. "And for the head's up about Tuesday."

"Just promise you'll be there." He turned to leave.

"You can count on it."

~~~~~~~~~~

"So, what did you think?" Ella asked as she parked around the corner from Morgan's place.

"I think you're wonderful, and Lester is quite the jokester, and I really like your station family." She pushed back against the seat.

"They make life a little easier." She turned the car off but didn't open her door. It was clear by her expression she had something to say. Her hands tightened around the steering wheel. "I know that he told you." It wasn't an accusation, as much as a statement, and Morgan knew honesty was essential.

"About Tuesday?" The day was all she could share because she didn't want to say the name.

"Asshole," Ella whispered to herself.

"Don't say that." Morgan reached to hold Ella's hand. "He cares, and so do I."

"It isn't like he thinks." She turned to face Morgan. "What Kay…" she paused to take a deep breath. "What she was to me isn't something that stops." Her voice was almost a whisper. "I know she's gone but being. . . "

"Being what, El?" Morgan praised the designer of the Buick Electra for providing the bench seat as she slid across and against Ella's side.

Ella shoulders flexed and then relaxed, surrendering to Morgan's gentle soul.

"You don't have to carry it alone," Morgan whispered in her ear.
~~~~~~~~~~

"For some reason, being with her on the anniversary makes the rest of the days easier."

Morgan wasn't sure what it meant to *be with someone* who'd died, but she could sense Ella disappearing into another memory. "Tell me what that means."

"Can we go inside?" Ella pulled the key from the ignition. "I'm going to be a mess in about a minute, and I'd like to do that in private." She looked at Morgan. "With you."

Morgan did something with Ella that she'd hesitated to do until this very moment; she took control of Ella's emotional care. She grabbed the duffle bag from the back seat, raced around to the driver's side door, and held it for the woman until she exited. Morgan continued guiding her as they walked inside the shop, through the back room hallway, and up the elevator. With each step, she reassured the firefighter, "I've got you, my love."

And she did have her–all the way to the bedroom, where she undressed Ella and slid a sleep shirt over her head.

"Will you let me be with you?" Morgan whispered.

Ella's head lay tucked against her breast, her strong arms limp around her hips. "I think I would really like that."

Morgan didn't need to see the tears to know they were there. Avoiding saying her name wasn't helpful, but giving space to the loss that haunted her love was what would get them through.

CHAPTER 14

Ella laid in the bed, staring at the industrial ventilation tubing running across the ceiling. On the job, she'd cut through ductwork like that many times in a fire, punched holes for smoke and flame to escape, while running inside to protect lives. She never thought about it as a sacrifice, only as a calling.

Something changed inside her the night of the photoshoot and the days that followed. Lester apologized for his discussion with Morgan but backpedaled to say that she didn't have to be alone in her grief. She'd heard him, but it wasn't him she needed. It was *her*, the woman wrapped around her torso with a leg hitched over her hip.

Everything was different because of *her*.

"Are you awake?" Morgan asked with a mumbled, sleepy voice.

Ella's torso trembled with a quick laugh. "I am."

It was Tuesday morning, Ella was awake before sunrise, and Morgan didn't know where the day would lead.

"I can feel you thinking." Her hand was splayed across Ella's abdomen, her fingers running back and forth over the muscular dips and peaks.

"After only a few months together, you can feel my thoughts?" She knew the petite woman was half sleeping, but the sentiment was sweet.

"Only about today, El."

Ella rolled to her side, so they were face to face. "I've decided that Kay would want you to come with me."

Nervously she asked, "Yeah?"

Their foreheads touched, and Ella whispered, "Yeah."

~~~~~~~~~~

"Are we walking?" Morgan asked as they exited her building. The sign on the door read *Closed* and would remain that way for the rest of the day. The rage room schedule was cleared, and Ella's rotation fell with her assigned the next three days off.

"We are. It's part of what I do. Will it be alright for you?"

She nodded, feeling confident she could manage this day. "I'll follow, and if it's too hard, I'll just be here." Her fingers tightened around Ella's hand.

"That means..." She fought the emotions.

"I know what it means, El."

They walked two blocks and stopped at a florist. Ella gave them her name, picked up a bundle of flowers, and carried them away. She never released Morgan's hand, not once through the entire transaction, and Ella felt anchored even with this burden of grief.

They passed hundreds of people, sidestepped trash and clutter on the sidewalk, Ella in the lead, Morgan at her side. The cemetery driveway was locked, but the footpath gate opened
~~~~~~~~~~

with a key. Ella had a key. It was one of the four on the ring with Charlene's.

"Private cemetery," she explained as she unlocked the door and let them inside.

Morgan nodded.

"You doing okay?" Ella asked. "I'm not walking too fast, am I?"

"I'm fine."

Ella's pace was slower once they entered the cemetery. She knew the path and stepped lightly as they crossed graves that held markers hundreds of years old. They stopped in front of a modest headstone, the name Whitlock arched across the top.

"Kay Whitlock," Morgan read, and the full name was finally spoken aloud.

Ella sat on the grass, fresh cut and green, perfectly kept over the space that held Kay. "Someone was here." She plucked the wilted flowers from the permanent brass vase. "Probably him, that selfish…."

She unwrapped the fresh flowers with more care than necessary at a graveside, and Morgan rested her hand at the small of Ella's back. This was a clear ritual attached to grief that didn't need an explanation; it just was. And so they each played their part in the best way. Ella held the roll of paper wrapping and pushed the decaying flowers inside.

One flower at a time, Ella placed them in the vase. "Your favorite color." She set the daisy in. "Your perfect memory." In went the pink carnation. This continued one flower after another, seeming like a random selection but each important to the past. The rainbow of color brought light to the otherwise dark place.

"I did this at her funeral," Ella explained, her eyes locked on the headstone and the bouquet. "Her church refused service and so did her parents, so it was me and the friends she called family."

Morgan sat beside Ella, an arm around her waist, not saying a word to break the moment. Ella was about to tell Morgan about Kay.

"They didn't come." Her head fell to Morgan's shoulder. "They left her, and she left me."

"I'm sorry, El."

Ella tapped at the flowers, probing them into perfect position. Emotions charged the surrounding space, but Morgan sat, waiting, and Ella could feel her presence. Ella knew the tears that came were not for today or even for yesterday. The tears were for all the tomorrows Kay had stripped away when she left Ella behind.

"I'm sad." Her voice broke the silence, draped with hiccups and tears. "I'm so sad that she didn't get to meet you."

Ella wiped the tear tickling her chin. For the first time, the cemetery felt peaceful, with the high walls of evergreen shrubs blocking the city noises and the hallowed space of forgotten souls. Ella let someone into the closet of grief, opened the door to possibility, and as Morgan held her, Ella believed that they could love each other through their best and their worst. It was clear to both of them that Ella would never forget Kay Whitlock.

Ella didn't know how long they sat in the grass. The afternoon sunshine was fading behind twisted, flowing clouds. The change in temperature made Morgan squeeze tighter to her.

"It feels like rain is coming," Morgan said, and seconds later, the first drops fell from the sky.

They were not prepared for rain in their cotton shirts and jeans, but Ella didn't move. She looked at Morgan and really saw her understanding as they let the warm summer drops wash over them.

Soon, though, thunder rumbled the ground, the vibration shaking Ella from her silent vigil. "I think that's a sign that maybe we're done here." Ella picked up the wrap and the old, withered flowers, carrying them with her toward the trash can at the exit gate.

Ella opened the gate and shook it twice to make sure they locked it behind them. Their clothes were damp as the sprinkling continued.

"Maybe we can duck into that store for an umbrella?" Morgan pointed at the shop on the corner, and Ella didn't hesitate as she held a hand over Morgan's head as though somehow she could keep her dry.

"Umbrella?" Morgan asked as they burst through the door.

The clerk pointed, directing them to the shelf where a single long-handled, cane styled umbrella laid. "It'll have to do."

The rain was falling harder when they exited. Morgan ducked beneath the umbrella, but Ella stopped and stood in the middle of the sidewalk, letting the water wash over her face. Her arms fell to the side, and she arched her back, taking every drop against her face and neck. Morgan watched, the most amused smile on her face, in obvious appreciation of Ella.

Ella saw her through the raindrops hitting her face. Morgan, sweet Morgan, so humbly strong and tender, soft and attentive; she was *exactly* what love looked like. Their eyes met, locked together in the revelation.

Morgan whispered, "Ella, you're so damn beautiful."

Captivated by the spirit of the moment, Ella's shoulders pitched. The umbrella fell to the ground, hands cupping Morgan's cheeks as they kissed in the rain, like a fairytale dream come to life. The world around them faded until thunder struck again.

Morgan's body trembled. Ella's did, too—perhaps from the sound but more likely from the adoring body against hers.

"El," Morgan said, the breathiness of her voice making Ella pause. "Oh, Ella."

"Let me take you home."

"Home" was a relative term for people who lived in fractured spaces. The massive dwelling above the rage rooms was hers, but she always wanted more. A little table here or a cabinet there, repurposed doors to create the perfect studio. But it never was. Things don't make a house a home, and as they rode the elevator to the second floor, soaking wet from the rain, Ella's hand hooked to her hip, she knew what home could be.

"You're shivering." Ella's hands rubbed up and down Morgan's arms, attempting to warm her.

"So are you." Morgan's teeth clattered.

"But I'm a firefighter. I'm accustomed to being wet and uncomfortable."

Morgan's lips trembled as she tried to play it off. "Uh huh, and I'm just getting a chill."

"Sweetie, your lips are blue." The elevator stopped, and Ella scooped her in her arms, carrying Morgan to the bathroom and setting her down. "Take all of that off." Her hand waved, pointing from shoulders to shoes, and she walked to the bedroom to get dry clothes.

"I'm not obsessive," Morgan said through chattering teeth as she thought about the neat rows of folded clothing in every drawer. Hopefully Ella would grab the easiest things from the foot of the bed and bring them to her. Morgan kicked out of the wet clothes and draped them in the bathtub.

Ella tapped on the door. "I've got some…"

"You can come in." Morgan shivered, wrapped in a towel.

Her wet shirt and pants made a dripping sound in the tub and outside on the fluffy bathmat below. Even though she was invited in, Ella's eyes were everywhere but on Morgan.

"El," her voice whispered.

"I'm not sure I should." She thrust her clothing-filled hands forward, but Morgan didn't take them. She pushed the bundle aside and stepped into tentative arms. "Morgan, I'm not…"

It was everything about this day: the memories, the rituals, the routines. Morgan was beginning to understand the sacrifices of loving another. That the last five years of grief would demand the day's attention, and as cold as she was, she was here. She was present as the mighty, but small, force that tilted Ella's world.

"You don't have to be anything for me, El." Her finger touched nervous lips.

Ella held tight to Morgan.

There was a new understanding between them. And Morgan felt calloused hands closing against soft cool shoulders. "If I asked you to touch me, would you?"

Ella's breath hitched. "I would do anything for you."

Morgan believed it, standing naked all but for the modest towel tucked against her breast. "I have never felt as safe as I do when we are together, and I have never wanted anyone more than I want you, but I don't want regrets, and I don't want you to be–"

Lips crushed together and hands cupped hips as Ella picked her up and lifted Morgan to the bathroom dressing table. Morgan's heart raced, hammering hard with excitement as Ella settled into the gap of her legs. Thighs tightened, and the heat between them spiked as Ella touched the towel's tucked knot on Morgan's chest.

Morgan nodded consent, and the towel fell away. Ella's lips touched the curve of Morgan's jaw. Featherlight, they traveled down an arched neck, across a hollow collarbone, and paused above the heaving, delicate flesh between Morgan's breasts.

Morgan held Ella's hand, pressing it against her heart. "Can you feel that?"

"I'm feeling a lot of things right now, and your heart racing is not helping any of it."

Ella's hand moved over her breast, tickling the soft skin against her fingertips. "Yes," Morgan hissed as her body arched into the touch. "Please El."

The sound of her plea, the desire in her eyes, Morgan wanted her, and she knew Ella was aware what a precious gift it would be. Touching and being touched was more than sex or pleasuring in the moment.

"Take me to bed," Morgan whispered, and Ella's hands slid under her thighs as she picked her up and walked them to her room.

Ella lowered them to the bed, hips tight against her as she slid between Morgan's thighs. Lips met, tender at first, until Morgan nipped at her. The moan that followed could have been her own, but when Ella's kisses moved down her chin and along the pulse point of her throat, she could hardly form the word to beg for more.

"Yes."

Ella arched to lean back on her calves and seconds later, her shirt was gone and the buttons on her jeans popped one at a time. "I want to feel you against me," Ella said, her shining eyes expectant.

Morgan's hands held tight to hips as they lowered against her. The intensity of their kisses grew as skin contacted skin. Lips rolled across Morgan's nipple, Ella's teeth closing, light and hard, just enough to cause an eager gasp for more.

"Yes, Ella. Oh god yes," Morgan whispered, pleading as her fingers tangled in the back of long dark curls, teasing her, breath catching, breasts arching to coax the journey down her body.

Ella didn't tease as the nipple released from her lips, caught in the energy of Morgan's pleasure. Kiss by kiss, rib by rib, she traced, mapping the freckles and marks. Morgan didn't shy away when a fingertip caressed the scars on her hip. Lips came next, and never in her life did she believe being touched would bring such delight.

"Can you feel me?" Ella asked as her tongue danced across Morgan's hip, nipping the curved flesh, and stopping to kiss her belly.

"I feel it. You." Morgan's shoulders pushed hard, arching into the mattress. "Please, please, don't stop."

Ella's head dipped close, her tongue peeking through to find Morgan's center. "You're so wet."

Morgan's thighs parted. "Of course I am, Oh," she gasped. "Look at you."

"I want to taste you."

"Oh, yes, El, Please."

Her fingers clenched in Ella's hair, guiding the woman to her sex. Ella vanished in her exploration of Morgan's body, tongue dipping deep, over and over, her face lost in the scent and taste of this new love. Her knuckle brushed Morgan's inner thigh, moving to unshaved sex and entering Morgan first with one finger, then pulling out slowly to enter with a second. Morgan begged for the touch, muscles torquing for more.

Ella was in no hurry, touching, tasting, waiting for Morgan to respond, muscles clenching, moans guiding, listening to everything with one goal in mind: to please the woman beneath her.

"Oh Ella, I'm going to..." Morgan gasped and nonsensical things came out of her mouth. "Yes. It's my—Yes, there. I can't believe...You are..."

"Tell me, Morgan." Ella didn't hide the satisfaction in her voice as Morgan's body tensed, muscles fading and clenching as the orgasm tore through doubt and fear, ripping at barriers piece by piece. She could love this woman forever. She wanted to be here with her for always.

Arms dropped, legs fell limp, and hitched gasps filled the space between them. Morgan's voice was breathy. "Come up here and let me touch you."

Ella was slow, moving from Morgan's center to her lips, kissing each of the new found spots on Morgan's body until she stopped to return to her hip.

"You're so damn beautiful." The vibration of the words tickled Morgan's belly. "Gorgeous." She licked the silky flesh near her nipple. "You taste…" She licked the hollow of Morgan's throat, and the gasp that followed was the reaction she needed. "Delicious."

"You have to let me touch you." Morgan pulled dark curls into her fingers as she grabbed Ella's neck, bringing her closer for a kiss. The moan of pleasure ramped Morgan's need to touch the woman by her side. "Your turn."

She tried shifting her weight to roll Ella on her back, but the resistance made her pause, bringing awareness that the fog of orgasm left behind. "Ella?" she asked, and dark eyes stared back. "Tell me?"

"It's not going to take much." Ella turned on her hip, naked from the waist up, button fly wide open.

Fingertips traveled across muscled shoulder, down the tight skin of her chest, stopping to tickle her breast. "I want to touch you?"

"You did, and you do." Ella arched into the hand caressing her breast. "Yes."

"I want to love you forever, do what you did for me." Morgan was dizzy from Ella's touch, satisfied in a way she wanted to experience again. Her hand slipped inside Ella's briefs.

"You give me everything I need and more." Ella hissed, her arm wide, encouraging her lover to move deeper. Morgan felt the clench of orgasm as Ella released into her palm.

Morgan's hand flexed to move, but Ella held it there. "Stay, just for a few more seconds. You feel so good."

Morgan chuckled. "I barely touched you."

Ella opened her eyes, staring into Morgan's. "Oh, you just don't get that you touched me more than you'll ever know."

Morgan nuzzled into the arms of the woman laying naked from the waist up. Her fingers traced tiny circles over the ripples of her ribs, across her abs to rest in the open triangle of her jeans. Fingers tickled the hairs, and Ella's gasp brought a tight squeeze to stop the next move.

She reached for the hand in her jeans, and her voice was strained as she said, "You are deliciously naughty."

Morgan smiled. "You want a little bit more of that?" Their palms steepled together.

The reply was absolute and also nonsensical. "Definitely. Definitely. Definitely."

CHAPTER 15

"Probie, you're with Feller," Ella yelled from the doorway as the alarm blared. She was in the middle of a walk-in call, helping a senior member of the community with their smoke detector exchange program. She was on the desk today, which was normal for her after the anniversary of Kay's death.

"Roger that," he yelled back, and seconds later, the trucks rolled out.

"That's a big fire, huh?" the old man asked.

"It is."

He put the new smoke detectors in his rumpled grocery bag. "Bet you'd rather be out there." He tipped his head toward the empty bay.

"That's my job." She looked at the phones on the desk. "And so is this."

The man thanked her for the help, and a few minutes later Ella sat at the desk, monitoring the alarms called on the warehouse fire. It was the second in this industrial park, and patterns like that usually meant arson.

~~~~~~~~~~

"Your Probie is good," Lester said as they sat together in the kitchen at the station house. "You did a great job with him." He pushed the coffee mug away from him as he stood. "You'll make an outstanding leader one day, Cinder."

Ella didn't know what to say. She loved her job, loved the commitment to safety and care for the community, but to know she'd passed that passion on made the rare moments of self-doubt fade.

"Thanks, Les."

"I mean it." He walked to the sink to wash his cup. "So that roll-out yesterday. That was the second fire in that park. Inspector needs a few of us out there, and I want you to go."

"That's not really my area of expertise." She argued.

"It's also not a Soot asking Cinder." He tipped the cup over in the drying rack.

Ella recognized his lean against the counter as an obvious attempt to put space between them. The move made her wonder. "What's that all about?" She wasn't trying to fight his order, but it also felt like removing her from what she knew best.

"Alonso Franco made the request."

She stopped, her jaw dropping open as she stared at him. It had been a very long time since anyone had mentioned his name. "What's that asshole want with me?"

"He wants your help, and maybe, just maybe, he needs some closure."

"No, I'm not spending time with him."

Lester wiped the counter near the drying rack. "It's not a request, Eastman."
~~~~~~~~~~

She walked away without another word, pissed about missing the fire call and doubly pissed that she had to be part of the inspector's investigation. "Fucking Alonso."

~~~~~~~~~~~~

"It's arson. This line here." He directed a laser pointer at the char around the door frame. "Fire doesn't move that way unless there's an accelerant."

"Right." Ella knew all of this. For the last hour they'd walked the building, and she'd listened to him explain fires and fire starting to her. She hated this guy, not only for his arrogance but for his ability to walk away after Kay's death.

"The report's going to be like the fire two blocks over."

Ella stepped over the debris, still soaked through from the water released by the fire hoses. "I was in that one. That fire was definitely no accident."

"That's what I said." His tone was biting.

"So why am I really here, Al?" She stood outside the steel frame that once held the entrance doors, her arms crossed over her chest.

"Your experience." He scribbled notes on the clipboard in his hand.

"Bullshit!" she yelled and ducked under the caution tape.

He followed. "What do you mean, bullshit?"

She walked to the parking lot across the street and turned to face him. "We haven't talked since she left." She stopped in front of Charlene. "Not one call, not one letter or message."

"Left!" He yelled. "She didn't leave Ella. She fucking killed herself."

Sweat collected on her forehead, rage warming her cheeks. "I know how she died." She pointed at him. "You..." She stopped herself from screaming words that could never be unsaid.
~~~~~~~~~~~~

"She was gone, Ella. Long before she tied that rope. Long before she did what she did."

Her back rested against the car. "Why am I here, Al?"

He stared at her, and it was obvious he struggled with the next words. "I've met someone."

Ella looked at him. For the first time in all these years, she studied his face. His eyes had a shine, maybe hope or peace. His posture was upright, the submissive slouch absent from his being. He was different, and his ability to move on was one more door closing on her memories of Kay.

She fished in her pocket for the car key. "I hope you'll be happier."

"Ella, wait!"

She couldn't hear another word as her foot pumped the gas, and the engine turned over. She didn't need to know about him or about what was missing because it wasn't her life anymore. As she put the car into drive and pulled away from the curb, she couldn't look back to see his face. She wasn't going to do it ever again.

"Have you heard from her?" Lester asked her over the phone.

Morgan sat at the desk in her apartment. It was after seven in the evening, hours beyond when Ella should have arrived. "Not tonight."

"She shouldn't be alone."

"Why?" Morgan stood, her chair slamming the wall. "What happened?"

"The past paid her a visit, and I should have known it wouldn't end well."

"What did you do, Lester?"

"It doesn't matter. It was Kay's ex and—"

She heard nothing else as her phone flashed with a call from Ella. "It's her. I have to go." She disconnected to answer. "Baby, where are you?" Morgan's voice was gentle, loving, and filled with a tone that she wanted Ella to run toward.

"Kay." It was the only word she said as the sound of crying took over the call.

Morgan knew where to go, knew exactly where Ella would be. "I'm coming to get you. Wait there for me, please."

She looked at the clock on the wall, knowing that she could walk faster than a cab or car could take her to the cemetery. Her legs ached, and her pace slowed by the time she turned the corner near the gate. Charlene was there, unlocked, and the passenger door was cracked open enough for a booted foot to hang out.

"Ella?" she called, careful as she reached for the handle.

The woman lay across the front seat of the car, forearm over her eyes, her face mostly covered to block out the world.

Morgan raced around to lift heavy feet and close the passenger door.

"Ella, baby." She opened the driver's door and, with care, climbed in, lifting Ella's shoulders to her lap.

"I'm not going to be good company tonight." Ella twisted against Morgan, sobbing into her embrace.

"Where are your keys, love?"

A hand came up, the ring of keys dangling from her finger.

"I'm going to take us home."

Ella rolled toward the center of the bench seat as Morgan yanked the knob to slide forward so her feet could touch the pedals. The Buick was the largest car she'd ever driven, and she was especially cautious as she parked in front of the shop.

"We're here, honey."

Ella was silent, and Morgan was patient as she led her into the building, down the hall, and into the elevator. It was a feat, helping her six-foot frame to the bedroom, and it frightened her how little resistance Ella gave.

Morgan unbuttoned the flannel shirt, tugged the t-shirt over her head, and unclasped her bra. The buttons on her jeans popped one at a time as Ella kicked out of her pants. Morgan held a thigh length night shirt up, and Ella ducked into it.

Morgan moved to toss the clothes in a basket, and when she turned back, the firefighter was already tucked beneath the comforter.

"I'm never leaving here. Knowing that Alonso Franco is going to have his happily ever after is just too hard."

Nothing more was said as Ella pulled the blankets over her head to disappear into the darkness.

"Oh love," Morgan called as she shimmied under to lie beside her. "I wish I could make it all different. I really do."

They held each other in the dark until the air was impossible to breathe. Morgan took position as the firefighter buried her head against the petite shoulder. Giving Ella a place to be vulnerable, being held through the pain, was all she wanted to do.

<center>~~~~~~~~~~~~~~~</center>

"Do you want to talk about last night?" Morgan asked. Her eyes gratuitously passed over the woman, back propped against the headboard, bare thighs kicked out from the sheets. She was breathtaking and an easy distraction.

"If I said no, would you make me do it?" She looked into loving grey eyes.

Morgan laughed. "Depends?"

"On what?" Ella waved her to come closer.

"On whether talking about it now will make things better for you later." Morgan crawled across the bed to sit beside Ella.

"Alonso Franco requested my help at an arson scene." She blurted the words, but they didn't make sense to Morgan.

Morgan's brow raised in question. "Who?" It was this backstory that she knew Ella didn't want to share, this last connection to the relationship with *her*.

"Al was Kay's lover–common-law husband, I guess."

"Oh."

"Yeah, and there's history after." There were words, explanations that she could see Ella wasn't ready to say out loud. "He wanted me to know he has a new love in his life."

"Why?" Morgan felt anger rise at the lack of sensitivity to Ella's obvious grief.

"Absolution." She opened her palm, waiting for Morgan to hold her hand.

"For you or for him?" Morgan asked, unprepared for the flare in Ella's eyes.

She stabbed a finger into her chest. "I loved her. I was there for her. What she chose...how she left us..." Ella sat forward, every part of her poised to retreat from the truth she'd fought for years. "He won't get anything from me. He left me to

163

deal with the ruins of *their* life. All of her shit. He walked away. Every single one in her family left."

Morgan didn't know how to say what Ella needed to hear. "I'm sorry." There was nothing else. Suicide left questions unanswered and a lifetime of what ifs. Ella carried the weight of Kay's silence every day. "I'm sorry they left it all on your shoulders."

"What he said about moving on…" Her hands clenched into fists. "It pissed me off because something inside of me was clinging to a life with her in it, and she's not ever coming back."

"There's no time limit on grief, El."

"I wonder if she realized that the choice she made would haunt me." The tears fell as spit flew from her mouth and sadness morphed into anger. "Did she understand that I'd carry her suicide around for this long?"

"Sometimes there isn't thought about anything beyond the pain of now."

"How long do I have to do this?" She rolled off the bed and walked out of the room.

Morgan thought about the pain of not knowing, the ripping apart of what was true and what is the truth. Kay's suicide had locked Ella in an endless, crushing loop of sorrow.

Morgan found her standing at the kitchen sink, hands pressed on each side as tears fell from her chin. Her delicate fingers moved around Ella's waist as her head rested against her muscled back. Morgan wished her love could soothe the fractures of Ella's heart.

"I feel… I don't know how to…." Ella's hands covered Morgan's where they rested on her abdomen.

"Tell me." She felt Ella's deep breath.

"Before you found me, I went to the cemetery, because I was so fucking angry. Pissed at Al for living without her and even more pissed at Kay because I stopped living when she died. She left me, and I'm so mad."

Morgan coaxed Ella to turn around, taking the woman into her arms and holding tight. "She left, and I know it's very hard to understand, but Kay must have struggled for so long."

Through trembling tears, she whispered. "She could have talked to me."

"It's not always that simple, sweetheart."

Ella stopped resisting the comfort she needed. The choice to leave was on Kay, and whatever led her to that moment was no longer Ella's burden to carry.

CHAPTER 16

Two weeks after the confrontation with Alonso Franco, Ella heard that his investigation had moved to a third location involving station sixty. She was a professional, but she was also fine with avoiding his continued presence. Local law enforcement was on alert for the criminal starting these fires, but the truth was another fire could create the lead they were looking for.

"Station eight eighteen, Station eight eighteen all units, all units report to 3002 Fellows Way. Stations sixteen and two forty-nine are already on scene."

"Probie with me," Ella said, and they pulled on their turnouts.

Lester climbed into the alternate truck, and one after the other, lights hit and sirens blared. When they arrived on the scene, it was managed chaos, stations working every side of the building, covering entry and exit.

"Eight eighteen, you're on the North building," the scene commander yelled, and the team rolled their trucks around to that side of the scene.

"Wilson, you're on me. If my ass moves, you move too!" Ella yelled as she jumped out of the truck.

She was on the ground, hose yanked from the roof and rolling out to connect to the hydrant that Lester was close to opening. Wilson watched the swell of water inflate the fire hose. Ella hip tucked the nozzle and proceeded toward the door.

"Entry, go!" she yelled, and two station eight eighteen team members busted through the frame and wedged the door off the hinges.

With the full force of water blasting the flames, she and Wilson moved as one into the building. Point and sweep, they stepped together, heading through the North end. Flames were everywhere around them, moving in unnatural ways. She keyed the mic. "We need two more in here," she said in a voice too calm for the moment, but she didn't have time to feel.

Lester's voice came through her headset. "Eastman, we have civilians 20 yards to your west. Slow, caution with the building materials stored in your path. You're the lead, go."

"Roger that. Twenty to my west."

"Probie, you copy." They pivoted the hose and moved together through the heat of the flames and smoke.

"Roger that," he said, and she could feel the tug of his presence behind her on the hose.

One step at a time, they moved through the ravaged building, their vision clouded by the toxic smoke. Ella sensed the North side of this fire was beyond control, but they advanced.

"10 yards west, it's impossible to see. Are they in—" The fire rolled over and over, gobbling up everything in its path as it moved down the hallway, advancing as if it was intended to trap the firefighters inside. "Accelerant!" She turned the stream of water on the quick moving flames.

Ella felt the full weight of the fire hose. "Probie, you on me?" She looked over her shoulder to see Wilson stumbling backward, flames coming on him fast. He'd fallen in the liquid, which covered him from head to toe.

"Eastman to Feller!" she called, but the only sound was the hum of radio static. "Wilson, respond!" she yelled at her downed Probie as she turned her hose across the floor, spraying a steady flow at him and on the ground, rolling to smother his fully engulfed suit.

"Eastman to Feller, man down. Man down!"

She flooded the floor, walls, and ceiling, creating a one-way route back the way they'd come. The smoke was thick, and her choices were limited: carry out her man or advance to find civilians that could already be lost.

Ella shot another stream, sweeping water to clear an exit. "Let's go, Probie." The oxygen on her tank read sixty percent as she bent to put the man over her shoulder. She'd trained for this her entire career, and with flames climbing the surrounding walls, she side stepped back the way they'd come.

Her boots shuffled, careful to move on solid ground. "Eastman to Feller," she called once more, grunting through each step, hoping that someone was on the West wall rescuing those trapped inside. The flames crawled closer, the heat begging her to quit, expecting her to fail and fall to the fire.

She could smell it now, the chemical Probie was soaked in. If the flames caught up to them right now, she would be defenseless against them. The smoke was getting darker. Like a desert mirage, she saw Morgan's face, her smile, felt her heart pound at the vision of the beautiful artist, and she thought about never holding her again. She thought about Kay and decided in that instant she wouldn't give up, not on her love and not on herself.

Wilson's body weight increased, and Ella knew he was no longer conscious. "Fuck Wilson, you weigh a damn ton." Her steps slowed as the flames caught her leg. She dropped Wilson and pulled the fire hose back toward her until the nozzle fit in her hand.

She sprayed the flames on the ceiling, across the walls and around their feet. Wilson didn't move as she felt the heat against her pants. She needed to get them out now, but the water supply to the hose cut off, and she knew they were running out of time. The steel shelf against the wall collapsed, knocking Ella off balance, and she dove to throw her body over the prone Wilson to protect him. The steel sliced through her sleeve, exposing her arm to the dangerous level of heat from the growing flames.

She shook him. "Wilson!" she yelled, knowing this was the last push toward the exit.

"Eas—n d— —u c—py?" Lester's voice broke through.

"Feller, I'm five yards from the exit."

The smoke was too thick for her to stand, so she hooked her arms under his, leveraged them with her legs and dragged him through the flames. As the fire closed in, she had to rely on the technology of her suit and the strength of her body to get them out.

She heaved his weight, foot by foot, until her back slammed against the wall. The door wasn't where it should be; the ground wasn't wet, and the heat sucked through the open walls, She'd lost her way, gotten turned around after protecting her Probie.

"Fuck!" she yelled into the void. She'd followed her original path, she was sure, as the hose lay where they'd dragged it, flame and accelerant creating an unnatural line to follow. She hooked her arm under his armpit and crawled along. The cut on her arm ached. She felt the heat through the slice, but she had to keep moving. Two yards, she had to be close.

Ella saw the daylight break through the dense smoke. "Found you, you bitch. You're not taking us today."

Lifting weights was never about tight abs or sculpted arms. It wasn't about out-lifting Marsh or the boys in the gym who teased her about obsessive habits. It was always about this moment, about being strong when others needed her, about getting out and about always staying alive.

Her back fell against the door, the heat baking from her shoulders to her hips. The daylight was bright as she dragged Wilson away from the building and into the grass.

She ripped the mask from her face, tossed the collar over her head and repeated the motion on her Probie. Wilson wasn't breathing. His lips were blue, and all she could focus on was that he would not be lost, not today.

She unbuckled her jacket and began compressions to his chest, over and over. "One, two, stayin' alive," she said as her arms pumped his chest. She heard a voice behind her, felt an arm on her shoulder, but she never stopped pumping Wilson's lifeless chest.

"Eastman!" the voice yelled, but she kept on pushing. "Eastman!" he yelled again.

She was deep in the moment, knowing every pump was the difference between life and death. She felt a rib crack beneath the heel of her palm, and still she went on. "One, two, stayin' alive." Saliva webbed from her mouth as she repeated the words.

Lester's shoulder fit beside Ella's, and his hands covered hers as an EMT moved on the other side of Wilson's body.

"One, two, stayin' alive." She was singing it now, in a whisper to herself, almost in a trance, blood trickling through her own clothes with each thrust to his chest. "Come on, Wilson! Don't you fucking quit on me after I dragged your ass out!" She pumped his chest again and again until Lester nodded at the EMTs to take over.

"Eastman, give them room to work." Lester grabbed her shoulders, arching her back, pulling her to her feet.

"He's still down." She stood beside them, watching as they ripped through his turnouts, cut through his shirt, and applied pads for the AED machine.

"Nothing!" one of the EMTs said.

"Clear!" another yelled, and they both held their hands up in the air.

"Shocking!" The machine gave the warnings just before every muscle in the downed firefighter tensed from the electric pulse. The measurements of the machine maintained a constant flat line.

The EMT yelled, "Starting compressions!"

Ella's count began in her head again, zombie-like as she stood to watch. A stabilizing collar was velcroed around Wilson's neck, and a backboard was slid beneath him. The team was efficient, and seconds later, they rolled his body toward the ambulance, the smallest of them still pumping hard on his chest. Ella didn't move as sirens blared and the taillights faded from view. He was her Probie, and he didn't have a pulse.

The blood from her wound was no longer a trickle, and blood fell from the cuff on her wrist.

"Eastman, you're wounded." Lester looked at her face for the first time, saw the pale complexion and the lightless eyes.

"I'm good, just a scratch." She went down hard and fast, and Lester radioed for help. When a firefighter goes down, hands to help come from every direction.

"She said a scratch," Lester said as they removed her coat. "This is a nightmare."

She looked down. The gash in her forearm was eight inches long, and deep enough to cause immediate loss of consciousness in any other firefighter.

"See, a scratch," she mumbled, trying to roll over to stand.

"Stay down, Ella." He pushed on her chest. "Let's get some leads on her. This is beyond pressure. Tie it off."

Her blood was everywhere, and three minutes after Ella was stripped out of her gear and the source of her bleeding was found, she was in the next ambulance on her way to Blacktree General Hospital.

"Are you sitting down?" Lester asked her.

Morgan was not sitting. She was standing in her studio working on the pencil sketch of her favorite calendar firefighter. She'd barely heard the phone ring. "I'm not. What's wrong?"

"Sit down. Are you at the rage building?" She could hear a horn honking as he yelled, "Get out of the way." He was obviously driving and maybe a little out of control.

"Okay, I'm sitting," she said, starting to feel a little nervous. "What's going on, Lester?"

"There was…" He paused. "There was—"

Morgan interrupted. "Is she hurt?"

"Please get ready. I'm coming to get you. Meet me out front."

She slipped into shoes and moved to the elevator, everything after that a blur as she stood on the sidewalk waiting for Lester to arrive. *There was…* The words replayed over and over in her mind. Why had she interrupted, and where was Ella?

Lester pulled up to the curb with his window down. "Get in."

"What happened?" She was barely locked into the seatbelt when the car pulled away from the curb.

"She's alive."

And for a moment Morgan realized Ella not being alive had never crossed her mind. Her gasp made him aware that this was her first emergency with a loved one.

"We had a call. There was a building collapse, an accelerant, and Ella's Probie was trapped."

Morgan's hand covered her mouth, tears streamed from her eyes. "Wilson? Is he…?"

"It doesn't look good." He didn't take his eyes off the road.

"And Ella?" What had happened to her beautiful woman.

"She carried him out, wouldn't leave him, and I had to physically remove her from the resuscitation. She's wounded, and she lost a lot of blood. Any other firefighter would have fallen with that kind of injury."

"How is she now?"

"From the last report, Ella was still unconscious, but her vital signs were stable. Wilson wasn't doing as well. We took her to Blacktree General. The wound to her arm was deep, so she's in overnight for observation."

"But she's…"

Lester reached across the armrest to squeeze Morgan's hand. "She's going to be alright."

~~~~~~~~~~

The entrance to the emergency room was cluttered with firefighters and EMTs. Lester held Morgan's hand as they threaded their way through the waiting crowd. One after the other, each asked Lester what he knew, and his solemn head shake was their only answer.

They were there for Ella, but also for the probationary candidate who was taken in for emergency surgery to repair the puncture to his back and the burns over most of his lower body.

"Can you give me an update on Ella Eastman?" Lester asked the receptionist.

He looked like every other firefighter in the foyer, soot-covered and damp with perspiration from the field. The receptionist looked up from her computer and was about to say something when she noticed the stripes on his uniform.

"She's fighting the sedative in curtain eight." She pointed with her pen. "She's more concerned about the fireman in surgery, so we're waiting for a doctor to come in to perform the wound care. Blood loss in the field is a major concern, so
~~~~~~~~~~

they'll keep her overnight on an IV, and we're waiting to see if she needs blood. Not much of a surprise, but she's fighting that, too."

"Is there anything she *isn't* fighting?" Morgan whispered under her breath.

"Are you the girlfriend?" the nurse asked.

"I am," Morgan said.

"She's fighting us about that, too." She pointed toward the curtain.

Morgan turned to look at Lester. "I don't understand."

"Hospital policy is family only in the ER, but next of kin on this form says "Morgan Hail." Listed as "significant other." So if that's you, Ms. Hail, your extremely stubborn firefighter is in curtain eight."

The nurse stood to press the gate release, and Morgan didn't hear another word until she was standing in front of the curtain, listening to Ella fight with her doctor.

"I don't care what you suggest," Ella was saying. "I need the full use of my hands and arms to do my job, so I want to talk to the specialist before anyone else touches my body."

Morgan waited as silence followed Ella's outburst. "El?" she said before touching the faded blue curtain hanging from a series of beaded hooks.

"Morgan?" she called.

The curtain rippled as Morgan pulled it back, peeking in to see the undressed firefighter, soot covering her face, hair knotted with debris, tubes tangling her to the bed. But Ella was still the most gorgeous sight she'd ever seen. They'd connected her arm to an IV line, three bags pumping fluids into her body. Ella's eyes were dark, shadowed where the brightness usually lived. The injured arm was attached to an extended table, the contraption taped and tied to keep the injury immobilized, and a sterile wrap lay over the top.

"Ella."

Morgan stared, frozen at the sight but relieved to see her awake. And as combative as Ella sounded, it was all music to

Morgan's ears. Ella flexed her wrist with an immobile wave, begging the woman to come closer. Morgan threaded herself beneath the IV tubing to get to her girlfriend.

She whispered in Ella's ear, "Just tell me you're okay." The blood stains on the hospital gown were a sign of how serious the wound was.

"My forearm is, well, it's not good. And that fucking doctor says his repair will give me, at best, eighty percent function in my hand." Her eyes went wide as she spoke, clearly desperate for this truth to be a lie. "I told him I wanted a specialist. He said I needed to worry about infection. Shit, if I don't have one hundred percent, what difference will it make?"

Morgan wanted to climb in the bed, wrap herself around this woman, and make the injury disappear, but she wasn't a magician, and there wasn't a simple fix.

"What do you want, El? Tell me what to do."

Ella's eyes closed as she struggled with the pain. She flexed the damaged forearm, and her face paled. "Don't let that butcher operate on me. Not until there's a specialist to look at it. Promise me. Les, you too. I need to keep my fucking arm!" The medications dripping into her body were doing their job as the combative firefighter drifted farther from consciousness. "I do not consent without a second opinion." They were the last words before her head fell back, and she closed her eyes. The monitor on the wall beeped, steady and constant, as her vital signs flashed on the screen.

"Is she alright? What's going on?" Morgan stepped around the bed, moving close to the injured arm.

"She needs to go now. Waiting for a second opinion won't only cost her mobility, it might cost her the arm entirely." He clicked his pen as he scribbled notes on her chart. "I'm ordering her to an OR."

"No!" Morgan blocked him from examining Ella. "You heard her. Nothing happens without a different surgeon's opinion. I suggest if it's exigent, you find that specialist, and you do it fast."

The nurse came in seconds after the doctor stormed out. "You've got some guts."

"It's not me." Morgan's hand moved to Ella's thigh. "She's the one with all the courage."

CHAPTER 17

"You have to fucking tell me."

With the restriction of her IV tubing, Ella could hardly put up a fight, but she had enough mobility to flip the foam cup at the glass panel door, just missing Morgan as she slid it open. Almost twenty-four hours had passed since the fire and twelve hours since they'd rolled Ella from the operating theater to the private room on the fifth floor.

"I can't tell you anything," the nurse said, preparing the medications in the IV and switching out the empty pouch of liquid for a new one. "They're still in surgery."

Ella thought it was a lie, that they were keeping the tragic outcome from her to prevent a setback. After the fight for her choice of surgeons, she didn't have a lot of faith in the medical staff. "Morgan, please, tell me how Wilson is?"

She was silent as the nurse poked the bag, flipped the dial to stop the flow, and bled any bubbles from the line. When the nurse finished and they were alone, Morgan leaned over the bed to kiss her firefighter. "Hi. What they're telling you is true, honey. There are about a hundred firefighters and some other people out in the waiting room hoping for the same answer, but there's nothing, not yet."

"Is Les here?"

Morgan shook her head. "He left a few minutes before your cup launch. The specialist came to speak with me, and Les was there, too."

"What did the specialist say?"

This was the million dollar question. Would Ella recover with full use of the arm and, most importantly, the full use of her hand?

Morgan smiled. "Surgery went well."

"What else?"

"El, it's too soon to know."

Ella looked at her immobilized arm, strapped to a splint that locked her in place from hand to shoulder. Her right arm was tethered to the IV drip, and monitor wires snaked out from beneath her gown. She was held captive, stuck in one position, and she hated it on every level. Her body felt foreign, helpless, and she was uncomfortable all the time.

"I want to get out of here," she groaned. "I fucking hate hospitals."

"Hey." Morgan's voice was soothing, a shelter in a storm. "I've got you. I'll stay with you until they kick me out." She hesitated as her hand moved to hold Ella's.

"Don't be afraid." Ella raised her hand enough for Morgan to tuck beneath it. "You won't hurt me."

The screeching of the chair across hospital linoleum startled both of them. They'd been so wrapped up in each other that they'd missed the doctor's return.

"Ms. Eastman. It's good to see you awake," the woman said as she stepped closer to the bundled arm.

"Dr. uh...I don't remember."

Ella's shoulder bunched with a horrible attempt at a half-shrug. The cringe of pain caught her breath, and Morgan was hovering beside her.

"El?"

"I'm good." The IV tangled as she gave a thumbs up.

"It's best to be still for the next twenty-four hours." The doctor silenced the monitors, beeping and jerking in response to the stimulus of pain. "It's Dr. Gorsey, as a reminder."

"Okay, Doc, give me the good news."

Ella and Morgan sat, listening, hands squeezing tight as the doctor spoke about the long road to recovery.

~~~~~~~~~~

"She said *how* long?" Lester was leaning against the open doorway, half in and half out of the door. It was clear he had the same aversion to hospitals that Ella did.

"Six weeks before I can do anything." Ella sighed. "No lifting, no carrying, no pushing. Basically, I'm a potato."

The tether of the IV snaked over her shoulder. but only one bag of mystery fluid was connected. She was close to the estimated twenty-four hour post-op evaluation, and she was itching to get out of here.

"Six weeks and then what?" he asked.

"Rehab, therapy, evaluations, whatever the specialist decides. I'm at their mercy now." Her half laugh was biting and lacked humor.

"You going to be able to get around at home?" he asked. "Or do you need–"

"She's not going to the cottage," Morgan interrupted, carrying two cups of steaming liquid. "She's coming to stay with me."

Lester smiled and winked, obviously delighted by the idea.

Ella bit back. "I'm in this contraption; don't throw your winks at us."
~~~~~~~~~~

"Hi." Morgan kissed her, feeling more confident as her girlfriend every hour. "I didn't have to smuggle the coffee, but take small sips to see how you feel."

Nurturing Morgan was even more beautiful than independent artist Morgan, and Ella felt protected like never before. It was Morgan who'd fought to keep the ER intern away from the forearm tear, holding out for the specialist to arrive, potentially saving her future in the department. If she didn't understand love before the injury, she understood it now.

"How about my luck, Les? I get to stay with this gorgeous woman." Ella relaxed in Morgan's presence. "She fought the whole hospital for me."

"I was there, Cinder." He poked at the IV bag. "Is she still on painkillers?" He stepped closer to the door.

Morgan nodded. "Yes, it's a little bit like truth serum." She turned to look at Ella. "We all know that you would have done the same thing for any of us."

"Uh huh, but if I didn't already know how you felt about me before the injury, I'd be damn sure of it now."

"She's kinda adorable like this." Morgan leaned in for another kiss, checking to be sure Ella could hold a cup before she gave her the coffee.

"Bless!" Ella said as she raised the cup to her lips. She set it down and looked at the man hovering at the door. "What gives, Soot?"

"Ah, Cinder, I think you scared me on this one." He was almost standing in the doorway.

"Man, it's just a scratch."

Lester and Morgan gave her a look, but he spoke first. "Nine staples and thirty-six stitches. That's not a fucking scratch, Ella." His hand clenched the door frame as he turned to go.

"Don't leave because I can't chase after you, and I need to know how you feel."

It was obvious something frightened him, and Ella wondered if it was Wilson and his youthful bravado that was causing the frustration.

"Your scratch?" he began. "You nearly bled to death because while you were pumping his chest, your blood was running out all over him and the ground." He kept space between them. "When they took him away, you went down." His voice changed. "Do your ribs hurt?"

She hadn't complained about the bruising or the ache in her chest, but she knew he could read the look on her face.

"The bruised ribs? That was me, and Peters from forty-nine," he told her. "When you went down, we had to start your heart."

"I didn't know. I don't remember."

"You wouldn't have because you were honed in on Wilson. Fuck Ella, anyone else would have died from that." He pointed at her arm. "You don't get it. Do you?"

"He was my responsibility." She tried to sit forward, and the motion drew attention to all nine staples and thirty-six stitches. "Damn, uh." She closed her eyes, trying to breathe through the pain.

"Inside!" Lester raised his voice. "Inside, you never leave a firefighter, but outside is another story because we are a team. We don't need to lose two."

The room went silent as Ella's eyes shot open, razor sharp in clarity as she misinterpreted the words he said. "Is he gone?"

"They airlifted him to the burn center."

Morgan's face went pale as she sat back in her chair.

Ella noticed immediately. "Are you alright, Morgan?"

She nodded. "I'm fine. I'm just very familiar with the Blacktree Burn Center." She looked down at her legs. "I spent a lot of months fighting to keep the use of my legs. They have an amazing group of specialists, but it's not a place I want to visit any time soon."

"I know." Ella reached for her hand. "I won't ask you to come with, but I'll need to go."

"He's in critical condition, Ella." He paused to look at Morgan. "I'm sorry to say this, but his legs are…If he survives, there's little chance he'll walk."

Ella's head turned toward Morgan, shutting out everything else. Grey eyes weren't visible behind closed lids, but her tears were. Every falling tear wrecked the firefighter.

"Dude." Ella glared at him. "That's enough. We can talk about this when I'm home." Her head tipped toward Morgan.

"Yeah, I got you." He waved a gesture toward his ear, making a phone with his thumb and pinkie finger. "Call me when they spring you." He backed out of the room, grabbing the handle to close the door behind him.

"I'm sorry you had to hear that," Ella said. She looked like she wanted to hold Morgan, but there was nothing more she could do, trapped in the bed.

"A fucking firefighter," Morgan said, the words not directed at Ella but at the universe around her. "I had to fall in love with a fucking firefighter." Her hands cupped her knees as she pulled up into a ball in the chair beside the bed.

"Fucking firefighter? I guess I've been called worse."

Morgan's head snapped up, staring at Ella and realizing what she'd been thinking had come out of her mouth. "Fuck, that's not what I mean. Damn it, El. How am I supposed to love you and like any of this?" She waved at the wounded arm.

"I've been doing *this* for ten years. This is the first time I've ended up in the hospital." If Ella intended to offer comfort, it had the opposite effect on Morgan.

"This time, but what about next time?" She wrapped her arms around her knees as she scrunched in the chair.

"The team takes care of each other. We train to get in *and* get out."

"I know that, but what if?" Her chin dropped to her knees as she stared at the frustrated woman.

"Morgan, life is all about what ifs." She held her hand out, flipping the IV tube aside so Morgan would touch her. "What if I wasn't cocky enough to approach you at the convention? Huh?" She held up a finger to stop Morgan from answering. "What if you'd said no to the Sage? Right? What if I hadn't gone to rage at the shop with Les? What if you'd never kissed me in the rain?"

"Ella." The whispered name. The fragility in her tone was heartbreaking.

"It's taken everything I have in me to let myself love you," Ella confessed..

Morgan understood the way she felt because she felt it too. "I know."

"Life is full of risks."

"Maybe so." Morgan squeezed her hand. "But most people don't run toward them."

~~~~~~~~~

"Ready to bust out?" Morgan asked as she dropped the clothes at the foot of the bed.

"So damn ready."

The discharge papers were on the rolling table beside the prescription forms and instructions for wound care.

"Help me out of this, please?" Ella was tangled in the hospital gown.

"It might be easier to wear it home, maybe, so you don't have to fit the shirt over the immobilizer?"

Ella's hospital stay had been extended from two to six days. On the second day, she spiked a fever, and they had to go in to remove infected tissue. The surgeon was confident the additional twelve stitches and three staples would not increase the risk to mobility. Ella was skeptical, but after four days of additional antibiotics and wound checks, healing was progressing.

"I know it would be easier," Ella said, "but I want to feel like I'm not a patient."

The bruise on the back of her hand was dark and rimmed with yellow. Removal and reinsertion of the IV on day two left her impatient when they'd removed the IV for the last time this morning. Free from the tether she was ripping at the snaps on her left shoulder, ready to escape this prison.
~~~~~~~~~

"Honey, slow down." Morgan grabbed her hand. "Let me help you so you don't pull—"

She was a second behind stopping Ella from snagging the plastic on her gown and tugging it in a small but awkward direction.

"Fuck!" Ella yelled as the nurse came in with a bag for her personal belongings.

"Good morning to you, too," she said, her tone cool. Morgan could tell Ella's attitude wasn't scoring points with today's nurse.

"Yeah, sorry, just trying to get the heck out of here, no offense to you." Ella dropped her hands and let Morgan help with the snaps and ties.

"Would you like me to help?" The nurse stood in the doorway with a wheelchair just outside.

This was one fight Ella didn't want. She was wise enough to know that help to the car was a battle she couldn't win.

"Lester is in the parking lot." Morgan said. "I told him I didn't need help to get you into your clothes."

"He loved that, I'll bet."

Ella let the gown drop to her waist as Morgan threaded her good arm through the frayed cut-off button-up shirt. The red and black plaid screamed hard-ass, but Morgan knew differently. The immobilizer barely fit through the left side, and Ella smiled as she watched Morgan's fingers close the shirt over her bare breasts. Morgan's smile was naughty, and although she tried not to, her eyes lingered a few seconds longer before the last two buttons slipped through their holes.

"See, human and hardly painful," Ella said as she shifted off the bed so she could wiggle into sweatpants. "No shame in being comfortable for the rest of my recovery." Then she grinned. "Especially since I don't plan on going anywhere beyond your loft."

Warmth spread through Morgan's stomach and chest as she helped Ella into the wheelchair and pushed her out into the hallway.

CHAPTER 18

"Come on, the countdown has started." Ella sat on the couch in the loft, her feet kicked up on the table with a bowl of popcorn in her lap. "Ten, nine, eight, sev—" A hand came up from behind to cover her mouth.

"I'm getting drinks. Be patient." Morgan went back to the kitchen counter.

Ella had been out of the hospital for seven days. They'd immobilized her arm in a sling, drawn tight enough to strangle and keep her from using it. But it had been nice staying here with Morgan. Their days had leveled out in an almost monotonous way, with regimented wound care in the morning and simple walks to keep Ella from going stir crazy in the afternoon. The shop was busier than ever, and Morgan allowed her girlfriend to help with the lightest chores.

Ella was aching to go to the firehouse, to visit Les and to come to terms with the third arson fire in the area. It had taken two good people from station eight eighteen.

"Seltzer with lime?" Ella asked as she held up her hand to take the drink.

"Just like you wanted." Morgan sat on the couch.

Ella was excited to share this with Morgan. It felt like ages since they'd first met, bickering over *The Blasphemers*. But it also felt like yesterday. And now they were going to watch the show together.

They'd talked all morning about Morgan's lack of season two knowledge, and Ella'd joked about how sacrilegious it was to be a season behind next Sunday's season three premiere. Even though they'd both watched it months before, Morgan had to know all the ins and outs and character arcs of what came before it.

When Morgan sat down she noticed Ella staring at the frozen frame on the television screen. "Hey you got kinda serious all of a sudden." Morgan rubbed Ella's thigh. "What's up?"

"I was just thinking about something." She pointed at the fuzzy shot of the number seven, paused on the screen.

Morgan adjusted to look at Ella. "Oh yeah? What was that?" Her eyebrow raised, curious and visibly nervous about the serious look on Ella's face.

"It's an observation, really, but I seem to have a twisted connection with arsonists." Ella set her drink on the table.

"Now that you mention it, I guess you do." Morgan agreed.

"One nearly took my life." She tipped her head to point at her immobilized arm.

"And the other one?" Morgan asked, never taking her eyes off of Ella.

"The other one?" Ella's smile lit her entire face. "That one changed my life forever because it brought me to you."

"Totally twisted," Morgan agreed as she kissed her hard.

"Mmm, yeah." Ella struggled to form words and was content to rest in the moment of happiness.

Morgan cleared her throat to gain Ella's attention. "Are we gonna watch, princess?"

"You sure you're ready for this?" Ella asked.

"For the 'I told you so's'?" She shook her head. "Absolutely not."

"Come on, honey. I'll limit myself to once an episode," Ella joked as she popped a piece of popcorn in her mouth.

She hit the play button on the downloaded files. Ella owned all of the episodes, including the behind-the-scenes bonus features, in full high definition. Any super fan would do the same.

Morgan moved into the bend of Ella's uninjured shoulder and took turns feeding popcorn to Ella and then to herself. The speakers burst with the announcement. "Sit back and shut your blasphemous mouths! Episode one of season two is here." The customary rainbow countdown clock appeared on the screen. Seconds later, the Arsonist's flamethrower scribbled the charred title of the show on a brick wall.

~~~~~~~~~~~~~~

"That was so cool the way she torched the tunnel and captured the stalker." Morgan bounced against Ella as she reenacted the scene with enthusiasm. "And Bruiser with the yarn ball as a gag to shut the stalker up."

It was only the first episode, and she was already obviously out of her mind with excitement to watch the second one.

"Oh my god, baby, that was so good!" Morgan wiggled in her spot beside Ella.

Ella's smile was that of a satisfied girlfriend who was celebrating on the outside, but "I told you so-ing" on the inside.
~~~~~~~~~~~~~~

"Episode two." Morgan pressed the button on the controller, and the catchphrase played as the title burned across the screen.

"It's a good thing we started early," Ella said, and she watched as her girlfriend fell down the blasphemous season two rabbit hole.

There were sixteen episodes, and each had a five-minute interview with cast members explaining their take on bloopers and hijinks behind the scenes. Dracea Barnes was featured in the second clip, and Morgan was impressed that Ella had met her.

"Was she like that in person?"

Ella raised a questioning eyebrow. "Like what?"

"Hot as hell!"

Ella's smile was an answer. "She was very nice and honestly curious about my cosplay. Oh, and yes, she is definitely hot, but not as hot as my girlfriend."

"Good answer" Morgan paused the screen. "Is she going to be at the next palooza?"

"I'd imagine she will be."

"We should do a couple's costume." Morgan said as she rewound to the season two group shot from the opening scene.

"There's no way I could top last year's." Ella tipped her head toward her arm. "Plus, I can't sew with one hand."

"What about with three?" She wriggled her hands and fingers.

"Maybe we can do it with three," Ella conceded.

It was easy to let the episodes continue, Ella fully aware of what was coming, excited to watch Morgan react to each climactic moment.

"I can't believe I didn't watch season two." Morgan smacked herself on the arm.

Ella held her hand. "Don't treat my sweetheart like that." She kissed each finger and the back of her hand.

"Oh, I'll remember that." She nuzzled into Ella's body. "Ready for another?"

"What time is it?" Ella asked, trying her best to hide a yawn.

"It's a bit late. Maybe we should get you to bed?" Morgan set the bowl on the table.

For Ella, bed was not the intimate affair it had been before the fire. The combination of props and pillows made for a less cuddly environment, but they were making it work with a lot of love and a ton of humor.

"You topping me again tonight?" Ella asked as she stood from the couch.

Morgan carried the bowl filled with the empty glasses. "That is so tempting, but I think I'd rather be the big spoon instead."

The playfulness was a mask they each wore to get through the tough nights of sleep. Ella tried, as she always did, to be brave, but Morgan was there in the dark, having lived through that kind of pain as a child. Ella wasn't alone, and her gratitude for comradery created a bond they both understood was unique.

"In case I haven't said it…" Ella hesitated, watching Morgan turn to look at her, seeing the love in her eyes, the sense of commitment, knowing how hard it was to remember childhood pain. "I wanted you to know what it means to me… what you did in the hospital for this." She attempted to raise her arm. "I don't know how—"

Morgan's finger touched Ella's lips. "I love you, El. More than I ever thought possible. And I'd do anything for you."

"But, the—"

Finger touched lips again. "Shh, there's nothing. There's you and me, and that's how we'll get through. Okay?"

"Okay."

Morgan took hold of Ella's hand and led her to the bedroom. She unbuttoned the sleeveless shirt and dropped it over Ella's shoulder. Morgan undressed her every night, and each time, the exchange was more intimate, more gentle. She was certain for the very first time that she could be with Morgan forever.

"One more week." She tossed the towel at Ella. "If you screw it up now, I'll hit you with this sledgehammer." She gave the handle a swing and dropped it on the table.

It was their compromise. Morgan let her help in the rage rooms if she didn't lift anything heavier than that sledge. Ella, of course, pushed the boundaries of that compromise every chance she got.

"It's just a scar now." Ella rotated her arm to show the wide discolored stripe on it. The scar ran in a jagged line from the wrist bone up close to the elbow. It was impossible to hide, and Ella had no intention of doing so.

"And the muscles?"

"I hit the gym next week, and we'll find out."

"So give me seven more days?" Morgan pleaded.

Morgan pushed the cart through the door. Over the weeks of recuperation, Ella couldn't do much more than walk for exercise and to burn off her anxiety over how slowly she was healing. In that same span of time, Morgan gained strength as they walked together. It was an unexpected positive from the experience.

Wilson, the probationary firefighter remained in the hospital, critical and on life support. Infection was devouring him one organ at a time, and although he was fighting, a positive outcome looked impossible. Ella didn't talk about it. She couldn't, but Morgan knew it would come.

"I'll give you seven days if you'll let me be the big spoon again."

Morgan's giggle was mischievous because secretly she liked holding her lover. Ella scooped her in her arm.

"Don't you dare pick me u—"

Lips smashed against her own, and although the kiss interrupted the scolding, Morgan's feet remained on the floor. When they parted, she patted flushed cheeks.

"Good. It's about time you listened."

Ella's arm slipped down her back, and she held tight for the longest time. The rage room was mostly set with plates and vases, the usual for a group, but the lingering hug made Morgan arch away for a closer look at Ella's face.

"Hey, what's going on?"

Ella broke her hold and walked to the bucket on the cart. They filled it with nicked and scuffed baseballs, neon yellow softballs, and a few oversized clinchers. She picked up the ragged league ball and tossed it back into the bucket.

"I'm damaged." She flexed her forearm, the scar shadowed in the room's dim lighting. "I already know something isn't right."

Morgan wanted to refute her words, tell her everything she said was hasty, but feelings aren't right or wrong, they just are. Ella was baring her wounded soul, and Morgan had to let her say it.

"I've always been a firefighter." She picked up another ball and tossed it in the air. "What am I going to be if I can't go back? If I can't pass the physical?" She tossed the ball again, but this time Morgan snatched it from mid-air.

Morgan didn't say a word before she launched the ball at the vase on the table. It smashed to bits, flying everywhere. "We aren't there yet, El." She picked up another ball and handed it to Ella.

"What if–"

Morgan threw another ball, smashing a purple etched plate and cutting off her question. The shards flew in every direction, and Ella stepped in front of Morgan to protect her.

"You're a firefighter, Ella Eastman." Morgan placed her hand over Ella's heart. "In here. And this?" She took Ella's wounded arm and kissed the scar. "This isn't going to change that. I know it in my heart."

She turned once more and grabbed a ball. This time Ella grabbed one, too, and launched it at the three-foot vase. Morgan smiled as the anger on Ella's face eased. It probably felt amazing letting go of some of it after holding it in for so long.

"Go again." Morgan slid safety glasses over their eyes and tipped the bucket toward her lover. "Let it go, El."

There was nothing left to say as, one after the other, Ella pitched the balls at every object in the room. The glass crunched beneath their feet, and when the last ball struck the framed glass pane, Ella screamed at the top of her lungs.

"I'm here." Morgan wrapped herself around Ella as they slid to the floor.

Tears and grief, pain and fear, tumbled with every falling tear. Ella had nothing left as Morgan helped her to her feet. The six-foot frame looked defeated as Morgan led her from the room and to the elevator.

Beatrice watched the entire exchange from the camera and stared at Morgan as she turned and mouthed, "We're okay," then disappeared as the elevator gobbled them whole.

CHAPTER 19

"Light weights. He said *light* weights, Ella," Marsh scolded her. It was their first day back in the gym, and her first day unsupervised by her physical therapist.

"Hell, Marsh, I don't need another babysitter." She set the pin forty pounds lighter, and he moved in to reduce it by ten pounds more.

"Light!"

She listened, and as her arms flexed, she watched the muscle under the scar swell. "At least I can hold it."

"You'll be back, Cinder-Ella, and I'm gonna be here to watch every step, girl!"

"Did you hear about the news thingy?" She pulled the weight and held it at the end for a second before letting it down.

He shook his head at her, clearly disgusted by her downplaying the event. "Thingy?" He changed the weight on the machine as they switched positions. "*Focus on Courage* is hardly a 'news thingy.'"

She shrugged and stepped behind to spot him. "Wilson is never gonna walk again. I didn't find that crew in the building, and I'm getting some kind of award for courage. It's stupid."

"It's not, Ella, because you carried that kid out on your back. You were practically on fire while you were also bleeding to death, and you still saved his life."

"It's bullshit."

"Maybe to you." He paused to look at her reflection in the mirror. "But the world needs heroes, and like it or not, you are one. And waving your rainbow flag during that focus on courage helps all of us in the community."

"It's not heroic to do your job." She took a drink of water. "I was just doing my job."

"Excuse me." An unfamiliar voice interrupted their conversation, and they turned to see some young kid.

"Are you that fireman from TV?" He was staring at her, looking at the scar on her arm before bringing his gaze back to her face. "You are."

"I'm a fire*fighter*," she said, emphasizing the second half of the word.

"You're..." He paused and held a hand out to her. "Sebastian Wilson is my neighbor."

She shook his hand, well aware her gloved hand was sweaty, but perhaps his was as well. "I'm sorry about his..."

"Don't say you're sorry, ma'am. He's alive and maybe things are gonna be different, but he's still here, and that's because of you."

"I don't know what to say, man."

Marsh stood up so she could sit down. She was grateful for it. He must have seen her face pale and decided if she was going to faint, he wanted her closer to the floor.

The boy smiled at her, his eyes wide with awe. "Just... please...when you go back, remember that what you did was good. The people that love him are grateful. I mean it."

Ella didn't know what to do or say as the kid walked away. There were moments after the fire, after her memory returned, when she relived the crushing of ribs as her CPR kept him alive. Every second mattered. The carry over her shoulder, the drag through whatever accelerant the arsonist used to burn that young man's legs. After weeks of trying to save them, both were amputated, and the road to recovery had begun. His life in the field was over, but the rest of his life hadn't ended.

"You want to finish, or should we call it for today?" Marsh asked, looking at her in the mirror.

"Just give me a minute."

Her forearms draped over the pads on the machine as she stared at her reflection. She took a few minutes to process and then they returned to their modified workout. It wasn't what she was used to, but damn did it feel good.

~~~~~~~~~~

"Good morning. Welcome to R.A.T.S. Rage Room."

The voice came from behind a rack of shirts, a monotone response to the tingling bell above the gift shop door. Beatrice poked her head around the corner, and when she recognized Ella, she leapt toward her. Arms hugged tight around the firefighter as the squeeze locked her protein shaker inches from her mouth just as she was about to take a sip.

"Uh, hello." Ella felt the hooks on her duffle bag bite into her hip, but she let the hug continue. She had an idea why Beatrice felt compelled to do it.

The interview with local media had aired the night before, and although she'd consented to all of it, the three-minute segment had stirred a bucket of emotions. National news picked up the story, and after sleuthing around, they'd connected the dots to her cosplay win, and her social media darling status had jumped, with millions of followers bombarding her with questions and comments.
~~~~~~~~~~

When photos from her calendar shoots were uncovered, the LGBTQIA+ community latched on to their new hero, and preorders for the new calendar on the site crashed the server. Her life was unbelievably weird, and the only person she cared to see was somewhere inside this building.

"I just wanted to thank you." B's arms fell away, replaced by nervous flailing. "Morgan would never say it, but using the rage room in the interview? It was a ridiculously fantastic move. We're booked through until the holidays. I think your girlfriend is kinda freaking out." She pulled Ella toward the desk to show the monitor for room six.

Seeing what Beatrice was pointing to, Ella gasped. "She's going to hurt herself!"

Ella dropped the gym bag on the chair and went to find Morgan. The hallway was quiet, the calm before the one o'clock storm. When she pushed the door wide, Morgan was arched sideways, trying to lift a thirty-six-inch television on top of a pedestal of blocks.

"Holy shit!" Morgan screamed when Ella's arms and body came up behind her to help.

"Hi, baby," Ella whispered in her ear.

The two of them stood, Morgan catching her breath and Ella breath taken. They set the TV down, and Morgan turned around to hug her girlfriend.

"Hi," she said and stepped back to swat at Ella. "You scared the shit out of me."

"Glad to be of service." She pretended to tip an imaginary hat.

"What are you doing here?" Morgan tangled their fingers together and tugged them toward the door. "I thought you had your evaluation this morning." She looked at her watch, checking that it was just past eleven.

Ella followed Morgan toward the chair in the hallway. "Yep, did it." Without realizing, Ella rubbed the scar on her arm.

"And?" Morgan dropped into a chair, tugging Ella to sit beside her.

"Two weeks of desk duty starts next Friday and reevaluation after to get back out there."

She knew this would be the hardest part for Morgan. In the months since the fire and recovery, they'd lived together full time. Ella hadn't moved out of the cottage one hundred percent, but their lives fit nicely in that loft space. She hoped it was permanent, but she also thought recovery would take much longer. She didn't want to return to the loneliness of life before Morgan.

"So you did it." Morgan stood and stepped between Ella's legs, feeling muscled thighs tighten against her. Her hands cupped flushed cheeks as their lips touched.

"Yeah, I did it." Her lids were heavy with adoration from the kiss.

"Never doubted for a single minute that you would do anything less."

Ella's hands reached around Morgan's hips, and when she stood, the petite woman came up with her. "Your cheerleading made all the difference."

"Go team!" Morgan waved imaginary pom-poms and slid down the front of Ella's body as she let her go.

"That's us, a team."

Fingers tangled together as they walked to the elevator. Ella knew Morgan had three rage rooms to set before one o'clock, but they had time. And she wanted to make the most of it. Ella pulled the elevator doors together.

"How does it feel?" Morgan asked as she pushed the up button.

Ella thought for a moment, trying to put it into words. "It's hard to describe. It's like I was away but I wasn't, and the team, even Lester, was crying. I thought I'd be sadder than I am. After all those meetings and doctor's reports just to get cleared to work the desk?" She paused to clear her throat and stifle the overwhelming emotions. "The desk is important, but no one wants it. Today I wanted it because it means I'm really going back."

Morgan smiled at her, and Ella's heart swelled. "You are, El. You really are."

The reality is almost as painful as what I'd imagined, Morgan thought as she stared at the final firefighter trading card. There were thirteen images this year, even though the calendar would only include the original twelve months.

It was Ella's idea to include Wilson, and after visiting him at his home, they agreed that the Widows, Orphans and Fallen Firefighter's Fund would benefit even more after the news story blasted everywhere.

Morgan used an image she had with Wilson in the background, a candid shot she'd taken as reference during the professional photo shoot. He looked happy, at home in the station house, and she hoped her sketch captured that essence. The back of the card included information about Wilson and the courage and bravery of firefighters lost and injured on the job.

"That's a great sketch of him." Ella said, as she leaned over Morgan's shoulder for a closer look.

"He liked it." She closed the portfolio. "This is going to make a difference."

"It will," Ella agreed.

"So, what was that phone call?"

Minutes earlier, Ella had disappeared outside to take a call. "It was Alonso Franco."

"Are you okay?"

"It wasn't about Kay, but yeah I'm alright." It was also getting easier for Ella talk about her friend. To share happy memories and learn to let go of the way she died so she could celebrate that she lived.

"What was it—?" When she thought about it, she knew.

"They caught the guy." Ella shoved her phone into her pocket. "The fire that almost killed me, and Wilson? That shit we were drenched in? It was restricted by government regulations and some bullshit. They traced it back to a factory, and only a few people had access."

"So he's in custody?" Morgan felt a sense of relief, knowing the man was no longer free to do harm.

"Yep, no bond, and with testimony from me and Wilson, he'll never walk free again."

"How does that make you feel?" Morgan asked as they walked to the car.

"Free," Ella said after a moment. "It makes me feel free."

~~~~~~~~~~

"This makes me very uncomfortable," Ella said as she sat behind the table. Even with Morgan sitting beside her, her body was coiled like she wanted to run.

"Your fans are waiting, though." Morgan squeezed her knee under the table.

"It's been months since that stupid interview." Ella picked up the box and unloaded the contents.

Each of the fifty cases behind them held a hundred copies of the new calendar. Although this was nothing like the size of their Blacktree convention autograph lines, the people standing outside were for them, the baker's dozen firefighters.

"That stupid interview went global. There's a guy out there from Melbourne, Australia," Morgan said, and Ella dropped down in her chair.

"There's five thousand calendars behind us." Ella pitched her thumb at the pile of boxes.

"Aw, it's okay Cinder Girl. You won't get a cramp until number five hundred." Lester made a scribbling motion with his hand and laughed as he sat on her opposite side.

"Les, you promised not to poke the dragon today," Morgan teased and wrapped her arm around Ella's shoulder to pull her in tight.
~~~~~~~~~~

"What are you, her prince charming?"

Ella punched his shoulder, probably harder than necessary to make her point. "She's my princess, you jerk. Get it right."

"Hey, when you're done fighting," their captain yelled from the door. "I'm about to let the fan club in, so stretch your signing hands."

"This is the craziest thing." Ella elbowed Lester. "Don't you think?"

"Let's ride it, Cinder Girl."

~~~~~~~~~~

"Feeling pretty proud of yourself." Morgan kissed her girlfriend as she walked by.

"Suffering for my public." She clenched her writing hand open and closed. "To think I went through months of rehab just to get permanent cramps from signing boobs." Ella flexed her grip again while Morgan slid an ice pack across the kitchen counter.

"You make it sound naughty, honey."

"It was that woman." She tried not to laugh. "The sister of that guy from the convention. It's her fault."

"I can't believe you signed your own breasts. You couldn't choose a better spot on the pictures?"

"What my public wants, my public gets."

Morgan threw the kitchen towel, and it smothered Ella's face.

Ella sputtered as she pulled the towel off. "Oh, don't low my high, baby."

"Low your high?" Morgan laughed. "Where the heck did you hear that and don't ever say it again?"

"I read it in one of those queer romance books on the shelf in your studio." She winked.
~~~~~~~~~~

"You did, did you?" She swiped the towel from Ella's hand and wrapped her arms around her. "Did you learn anything else from all that reading?" Morgan teased.

"I may have learned a thing or two."

"Hmm, I like things."

"Oh yeah, I'm very well aware of the things you like."

"But back to quoting queer romance." She stepped far enough away to sandwich the ice on Ella's hands. "You need better material."

"What if I just quote my own romance?"

Morgan raised a curious brow, encouraging her to go on. "Gimme what you got, princess."

Ella smiled, and she paused, obviously thinking. "If I told you I never want to leave your side, could you live with me?" She set the ice on the table.

In contrast to Ella, Morgan wasn't thinking about the present as she processed the words. "Uh, that's not a quote from our romance."

Ella's legs parted. "What if it was?"

Morgan's eyebrow raised with a lightbulb moment and she stepped between Ella's legs. "Would you promise not to leave?"

"Cross my heart." Ella's finger drew a line over Morgan's chest.

Morgan giggled. "That's my heart, silly."

"It's mine, too." Ella's hands slipped to Morgan's hips, tickling under the hem of her shirt to touch bare skin.

Morgan twisted away from Ella's hands. "Hey, uh, no. Your hands are cold."

Ella didn't let go. "You know what they say about cold hands, don't you?" She leaned in for a kiss.

Morgan's words were breathy as she said. "I have an idea."

The kiss was featherlight, and Morgan's eyes were closed when Ella answered. "Cold hands, hot boobs."

Morgan's eyes popped open with disbelief. "You're such a smartass. That is *not* what they say. They say cold hands, warm heart. It's *heart*."

Ella flexed her hands again. "If you survey five thousand happy calendar customers, they might vote for boobs." She walked to the gym bag to remove a glossy finished calendar and unfolded the pages to reveal her month.

"It's not June yet." Morgan laughed.

"It's June somewhere."

"That's not how calendar's work, princess." Morgan patted Ella's chest as she moved beside her. After closer inspection, she laughed. "This is only June."

Ella held it up, tilting it for better light. She'd cut away the rest of the calendar pages, making it a sort-of Ella pinup. "June is all you need, baby."

"I thought it was love."

Ella put the calendar in place with the Blacktree fire department magnet. "That too, baby. That too."

If you or someone you love needs help, resources are available.

National Suicide Hotline call: 988

Hopeline: Text HELP to 741741
Anonymous text hotline

The Trevor Project : thetrevorproject.org
Call: 1-866-488-7386
Text: 678-678

SAMHSA National Helpline: 1-800-662-HELP (4357)
Substance abuse and Mental Health Services

American Burn Association: ameriburn.org

Thank you for reading the Sapphic romance Conned.

If you enjoyed this stand-alone story you might enjoy more of Sharon K Angelici's work.

The Maker Series

MARK OF THE MAKER (BOOK 1)

Wildwood Blackstone believed her dream of being a country blacksmith was coming true. When the town of Bannock hires her to restore their abandoned carriage house built in the 1800s, she can't wait to begin.

But there are more than ghosts in Bannock and shortly after her arrival she discovers this truth. When a childhood friend answers a call for help, Wildwood finds a part of her past that she longed to rediscover. Together they reveal Bannock's secret and uncover the Mark of the Maker.

THE MAGICK AND THE MAKER (BOOK 2)

Wildwood Blackstone longed for a life as a small-town blacksmith. She didn't imagine monsters or magick, and she never expected to fall in love with Shay.

Book two of the Maker Series finds the two women tangled together in the dark secrets buried deep in Bannock's small-town history. Is their commitment strong enough to carry them through? Who is the keeper of the Magick? When will Wildwood and Shay uncover the mystery behind the Mark of the Maker?

ORIGIN OF THE MAKER (BOOK 3)

Wildwood and her girlfriend Shay have uncovered Brigid's secret hidden deep in the earth.

Who is the stranger in the carriage house? How are they there? What do they know about the secret and the power it holds? Can Wildwood and Shay find the answers and keep fighting the monsters hunting them night and day? Find out in book three of the Maker Series. Origin of the Maker Coming in 2022.

LEGACY OF THE MAKER (BOOK 4)

In a secret world filled with magick, Wildwood Blackstone has encountered unbelievable mysteries. As the blacksmith in her new hometown, she's survived and endured the call to wield the hammer of the goddess Brigid, but to what end?

Celebrating a year with her girlfriend, Shay, the two continue their search for answers. What lived inside Andrea Peters? How did the entity survive for hundreds of years? Who controlled her all this time?

Their call to be The Magick and The Maker of Bannock comes with more questions than ever, but it might also come with answers to their past. Wildwood and Shay are drawn into endless realms, all of which lead to the Legacy of the Maker.

Rage Room Romance Series

Book 1
CONNED

For Ella Eastman, firefighting is life. She's devoted her body to being the best, but everyone needs a break from reality once in a while. For Morgan Hail, art is life, but she has to make a living. Their lives collide when television fandoms intersect at The Blacktree Comic Palooza.

Morgan's captivating fanart leads to a heated misunderstanding, and a cosplay contest brings these two women together–though only one of them knows the truth. This unlikely pair heats up when their real-world lives collide, but what will happen to their budding romance when Ella reveals her secret identity? And can they find a way to make things work when Ella's job hits a little too close to home? Conned is a story of love, loss, new beginnings, and fandom.

Book 2:
DECONSTRUCTED

After eight years, Ella Eastman has a plan to create the perfect marriage proposal for her partner, Morgan. Inspired by Morgan's to-be-read pile, Ella struggles to incorporate her favorite romance tropes while asking the big question. The ideas pile up, as do the failed attempts to create their once-in-a-lifetime memory. How do you give the perfect partner the perfect memory of a perfect proposal? For Ella, it all seems to come together quite imperfectly. Revisit the Rage Room Romance's chosen family as they unite for Operation Perfect Proposal.

The Alice and Violet Series

YULE BE HOME FOR SOLSTICE
Alice and Violet Book I

Violet and Alice's December road trip is definitely a trial by transport as they set out to deliver the perfect Yule log for the Solstice celebration. This cross-state drive commemorates twenty years of sapphic bliss and three hundred thousand miles on their Subaru Outback named Bess. What happens between home and Aunt Eunice's house is a romantic comedy of errors. Sit back and enjoy this *Planes, Trains, and Automobiles*-style adventure to deliver the perfect Yule log for Winter Solstice.
Available now in print, eBook, and audiobook.

DOUBLE DYNO
Prequel to Yule Be Home For Solstice
Alice and Violet Book II

On a two-week hiking and climbing tour, Al Hadley guides a small team toward high adventure. With her best friends PB and Britt making up the Extreme Adventure Group, the goal is to build confidence and experience for each client. What they weren't counting on was Violet Crest and her amateur adventuring ways.

Weeks of planning and detailed maps can't tame Violet's curious nature. She's determined to make every moment count by capturing as many as possible through her camera lens, testing the boundaries and the patience of AEG's team leader, Al.

Dig into the story before the love story, in this slow burn, opposites attract, adventure and the prequel to *Yule Be Home for Solstice*.

MORE BOOKS FROM SHARON K ANGELICI

DEAR KANE;
WHAT I WISH WE WOULD HAVE SAID

Do the words that we say in front of our children build them up or tear them down? This short story explores the consequences of hatred and bigotry when it applies, unknowingly, to someone that you love. There's a time in every relationship when a parent must let go of the dreams they have for their child, so the child can chase what they dream to become.

IMMORTAL HUMAN TRUTH

Immortal Human Truth is a collection of poetry written by the author as she traveled to promote her first book Dear Kane; What I wish we would have said.

Each section explores experiences with love, injustice, loss and triumph of the spirit.

SHE BELIEVED SHE COULD

What can you do in a single day? Why haven't you done it yet? Jump out of your comfort zone and dive into life as you follow the author on her journey to achieve 365 new experiences in 365 days.

ABOUT THE AUTHOR

Sharon K. Angelici, she/her, was born in the American Midwest, but her heart and soul belong to the mountains of Colorado.

She began writing as a child, using words to recover from trauma-induced depression. As a member of the LGBTQ+ community, she's an advocate for depression awareness and suicide prevention. In 2016 she published her first book dealing with both subjects, Dear Kane; what I wish we would have said.

Sharon is a full-time lover of life and all things Pagan and Magick. She's an artist and blacksmith, which inspired her to create her Maker series.

Written By Sharon K. Angelici